"When did you know you were a lesbian?" Montserrat blurts out.

"People don't generally label me a lesbian, they label me nuts. When I tell them that I've been in love with a woman for five years and that I went to bed with her only twice, they don't consider me a lesbian, they consider me nuts. She was in show business and..." Montserrat listens to Anna with complete abandon. On the other hand Anna fears that if the poor woman asks her next whether "you're born ... or you become ..." she won't be able to control herself.

Fortunately, instead of asking further about Anna, Montserrat prefers to state clearly what her feelings or fears are. "I'm scared to think of having a relationship with another woman. Once ... no, once was enough, too painful. No matter how much I sometimes ... No ... No way."

Anna has had it. Her response is immediate. "Well but Montserrat, in life you've got to be brave. Otherwise, look, you're not doing men, you're not doing women ... you'll be doing a lot of museums."

COSTA BRAVA

BY
MARTA BALLETBÒ-COLL

THE NAIAD PRESS, INC.
1997

Printed in the United States of America on acid-free paper
First Edition

Editor: LeeAnn Day
Cover designer: Bonnie Liss (Phoenix Graphics)
Typesetter: Sandi Stancil

Library of Congress Cataloging-in-Publication Data

Balletbò-Coll, Marta.
  Costa Brava / by Marta Balletbò-Coll.
     p.   cm.
  ISBN 1-56280-160-0
  1. Lesbians—Fiction. I. Title.
PS3552.A4677C6   1996
813'.54—dc21
                                              96-47131
                                                CIP

To Ana Simón Cerezo

About the Author

Marta Balletbò-Coll was born in Barcelona in 1960 and obtained her Master's Degree in Chemistry in Barcelona and her M.F.A. in Film at Columbia University with a Fulbright Scholarship. With her business associate Ana Simón Cerezo, Balletbò-Coll plans to keep making many more film comedies such as the next one: "Honey, I've Sent the Men to the Moon!" starring Desi del Valle.

Chapter 1

Barcelona has such subtly blessed weather that only the natives who have been away from the city for some years appreciate it. The rest of the natives constantly complain about its unbearable humidity. Today is a spectacular day. The sun shines, the temperature is compliant, and no wind blows. It is a great day to hang your clothes out to dry after the laundry is done.

Barcelona is the capital of a Mediterranean region called Catalonia which is administratively linked to Spain. One of Barcelona's landmarks is the Temple of the Sagrada Familia by the Catalan architect, and genius, Antoni Gaudí. The construction of the Temple began in 1884, but that does not mean that the Temple is now finished. For one to jump to this conclusion would be to not take into account the very own Catalan idiosyncrasy. Cranes, along with endless crowds of Japanese tourists, can be seen by the completed, huge towers of the Temple.

On a rooftop near the Temple of the Sagrada Familia, another Catalan genius is in the midst of a creative outburst. Her name is Anna Giralt-Romaguera and she rehearses a monologue titled *Love Thy Neighbor*. It is often said that the distance between madness and genius is as thin as a cigarette paper. That is why to call Anna a genius is not too wild a guess. This woman, in her late twenties, stands on the rooftop surrounded by underwear, towels, and colorful clothes which all hang from clotheslines. In fact, the entire rooftop is full of lines from which clothes hang.

Anna has two people working with her. One of them is Bill, a camera person who videotapes Anna's performance with a U-matic professional video camera, and the other person is Anna Jr., a young girl who holds the cue cards for Anna.

Anna plays the role of a housewife. In fact, her costume has been created to help communicate this idea. Her character, the housewife, works at the token booth of a subway station. She wears a blue uniform with a scarf placed around her neck with total absence of grace. Her makeup is even worse. One suspects that the housewife tries to apply to herself all of the beauty tips she reads about, and that she tries really hard. Probably, she even thinks

2

she looks really smart and feminine. The truth is, though, that her ideas about style and elegance are far away from the execution. The English language has a word that describes this particular housewife perfectly well. That word is tacky.

The most intriguing thing about the housewife is that one cannot help loving her. Her image shortcomings make her sweet and human; without them she would be an authoritarian working-class womb, mother of two and married to Carlos, and living in Barcelona.

Anna is about to tape the monologue right from the start. She wrote it herself and she is about to play the part of the housewife. A visible microphone hangs from Anna's skirt. She starts the monologue from outside the frame of the video that Bill tapes. For now, she just screams like a hysterical over-stressed mother would.

The only images seen through the camera are the endless pieces of underwear hanging on the lines, almost completely hiding the impotent Temple of the Sagrada Familia. Anna screams.

"Mónica! Mónica and Jordi both of you get out of the garden. Carlos! The kids are in the neighbor's garden. Carlos... Carlos... get the kids out of the garden. Carlos!"

She has a mind of her own. What she does not convey with words, her expressive long red fingernails communicate with gestures. She might not have many sophisticated ideas in her mind but the few she has, she has long nailed down and nobody will make her change. After the yelling, the housewife enters the frame. She speaks straight to the camera.

"No really, she's a new neighbor and I don't

want the kids jumping into her garden. Carlos! Damn." (She pauses.) "Well . . . the neighbor, she's a . . . you know, she's a . . . a *lesbian*." For some reason, the word "lesbian" is difficult for the housewife to utter.

She is on the rooftop to pick up the already dry clothes but it seems she cannot quite do it. Every time she turns toward the clothing to pick up a new piece of underwear, a new idea crosses her mind and she forgets about the underwear. She turns back toward the camera and she simply has to share it with everyone.

"I'm a very liberal person, I'm a communist! But I don't want the kids jumping into her garden, you know. What if one day they run into the whole female tennis Olympic team, eh? I'm a very liberal person but it's just that the kids, you know, could get some ideas." She goes back to pick up more clothes, but again, she does not conclude her action.

"The thing is that I'm a communist and my husband, Carlos, he's a socialist and we have our differences at night. But when we get together we say, 'OK, time out' and we put aside our differences and we . . . proceed."

All of a sudden, the housewife has a lyrical *momento*. "Sometimes I think that pleasure like that can't go on without some kind of punishment." She cannot complain as she further elaborates her point. "When the women get together at work and they start complaining about men . . . I have nothing to say."

In a quite definitive manner, she addresses the bottom line of her discourse. "Sex is great with Carlos!" What Carlos is not very good at is making the kids stay away from the neighbor's garden. This simply drives the housewife crazy. The housewife hears them playing in the neighbor's garden again. She gets very upset as she realizes it and she screams anew. "Carlos! Damn!"

Anna rehearses the monologue and videotapes it all so that later she can study her performance. Some thoughts cross her mind. "I've had enough of video-taping the rehearsals. It's time to make a good videotape of the monologue and send it to Another Stage, in San Francisco. If they like it they'll take me on the U.S. tour. Otherwise, I'm gonna spend the rest of my life working as a tour guide in Barcelona."

That is her real job. Anna works as a tour guide. She had been living in New York for several years. That is where she learned that your job is one thing and your career the other. Anna wants to be a playwright and she works now as a tour guide, as simple as that. Today is a gorgeous day and Anna is one of the Barcelona natives who knows how to appreciate this terrific weather.

Her tour guide uniform coincides with the one of the housewife except for the scarf. The uniform is a simple navy blue skirt and jacket combination with a white blouse. She wears high heels only when mandatory. More often than not she uses tennis shoes. The name of the company Anna works for is Costa Brava Tours. Anna Jr. is her assistant. Anna Jr.'s job is to hand out leaflets about the various tours. Advertising is crucial for this line of business.

Anna uses a red umbrella so every tourist sees her from afar. No other tour guide in the city uses an umbrella because they fear being perceived as ridiculous. Anna, who could not care less, learned the trick of the umbrella when she was in Washington D.C. A Washington tour guide worked with an opened red umbrella with a Mickey Mouse disguise on top of it, but to adopt the whole thing in Barcelona would have made Anna a serious candidate to enter the nut house. That is why she just uses the flashy red umbrella without the Mickey Mouse topping.

Anna wears a red badge with her name and the name of the company, and a red ribbon as a sign of solidarity with the AIDS cause. She has some kind of particular liking for red.

To an aspiring playwright/performer addressing a crowd of tourists is an excellent way of rehearsal. Anna has a real job and a very strong vocation. She is all set and does not need anything else in her life (or so she thinks).

The Barcelona tour given by Anna always visits the same spots. She gathers the tourists near the Temple of the Sagrada Familia on Gaudí Avenue, where she checks their names on her list. After that, they all get on the bus and they start the circuit. First comes the visit to the Columbus Monument located at the bottom of the Ramblas, Barcelona's wildest boulevard. The second stop is Barcelona's Cathedral and Antoni Gaudí's Casa Batlló and Casa Milà. Saint Paul Hospital and Park Güell, another Gaudí spectacular work, are the next landmarks to visit. They are terrific places to videotape. Anna generally allows the tourists some time to do so.

"OK everybody, it's video time. Shut it up!"

The last stop is the Arch to the Unknown Soldier. Anna checks her watch and she realizes the tourists' favorite moment has arrived.

"Twenty minutes for yummy yummy time!" Before she finishes the sentence, they have all gone. Where they put what they eat escapes Anna. They invariably start with a gazpacho and some *jamón* (ham) then a Valencian *paella* or a *"fideuà,"* which is like a *paella* but with noodles instead of rice. Then comes Catalan sausage with beans and finally the ice cream. All that is generously watered with abundant *sangria*.

After lunch, Anna summons them at Gaudí Avenue. She warns them that the best is yet to come. "I'm glad that you enjoy Barcelona. Wait until you see the Costa Brava. It's absolutely unbelievable."

She adores the Costa Brava. By now her audience is mostly females, because men are generally taking their naps in the bus. Anna checks her watch and she concedes to what many of the women desperately need. "OK now . . . potty break!" The relief on their faces is beyond description. They flee toward the nearest toilet.

Chapter 2

After work, Anna picks up the last revised copy of
her monologue *Love Thy Neighbor* at the photocopy
place. The covers are red. She cannot wait to get
home to glance at it. It looks really good. She passes
by one of the most prestigious independent theaters
in Barcelona. It is the SAT (Sant Andreu Teatre), a
kind of "Off-Off Broadway" outlet. They are playing
Oedipus Queen, starring Marta L. Puig, the Diva of
Independent Catalan Theater. Anna casually looks at
the theater's main door. It is closed. Every time she

passes by the theater, she gives that casual look and she always finds the door closed.

Anna's apartment is sunny like most of the apartments in Barcelona. She is painting the walls of her apartment. The process takes forever, as is usually the case. Painting the apartment is becoming not only lengthy, but also painful for Anna. Every time she moves furniture, all of a sudden photographs or letters from the past show up. Yesterday she found pictures of the lead actress in *Oedipus Queen*, Marta L. Puig. Those pictures Anna had long forgotten. In the pictures, both women are shown friendly with each other in a bar. The photographs now cover the floor of the apartment.

In one of her rooms, Anna has a flier of Costa Brava Tours displayed on a bulletin board along with an entry form for San Francisco's Another Stage, the U.S. international Lesbian and Gay Theater Touring Company. There is also a black and white autographed picture of Marta L. Puig. The dedicatory reads, "Anna, Anna, Anna..." and is signed, "Marta."

The telephone rings. There is a fax and telephone answering machine on the floor. Anna's outgoing message is of herself whistling Handel's *Hallelujah*. As Anna opens the door of the apartment she hears the machine record a message. The woman leaving the message has a delightful Puerto Rican accent.

"Hello Anna? Anna, this is Jesse, Jesse Piñeyro. You know Anna, I'll do the final videotaping tomorrow instead of Bill. I have an NTSC video camera and if you want to make a copy for San Francisco that's the one you need. Also, I have a copy of your play — I mean monologue — a copy of *Love Thy Neighbor*. If you need anything you should reach me at this number, area code 972 . . ."

Anna rushes toward the answering machine with some difficulty. Today she wears high heels. She picks up the receiver just in time. "Hi there, this is Anna."

Anna could not live without a fax. Her boss faxes her, everyday, the list of tourists who sign up for the tour which is why she needs the fax machine. She also receives application forms or information from theater festivals all over the world through the fax. That is how she got the entry form from Another Stage. Once again, job and career become perfectly integrated. With no further distractions in her life, she is convinced that she will be able to get whatever she wants in life. In fact, Anna has not had what she herself calls "personal distractions" for a long while. Other people call it relationships or casual sex depending on the distraction's duration.

The three women, Anna, Anna Jr., and Jesse Piñeyro, the Puerto Rican video camera operator, are on the gorgeous rooftop. They are determined to shoot the final videotape of the monologue. Coincidentally, the Cardinal Archbishop of Barcelona celebrates a mass in the open air. Around 5,000 people attend the ceremony, which congregates various choruses as well.

Anna Jr. holds, as usual, the cue cards. Jesse is a hyperactive woman living in Barcelona. Anna works with her with ease. Both Anna and Jesse stand by the U-matic NTSC video camera and try to decide where Anna Jr. should hold the cards.

"That's better. Leave her on that side. So when do you want the tapes in San Francisco?" asks Jesse.

"May 28th," answers Anna.

"I love San Francisco . . ."

". . . and Boston right? They say that Boston and San Francisco . . ."

"No, San Francisco." Jesse checks the camera viewfinder. "Is it for a theater festival?"

". . . but San Francisco is foggy. Oh no, it's for a U.S. tour. If that tape you're gonna make now . . ."

Jesse can hardly get to the viewfinder. "They always do these things for tall people . . ."

"Yeah, and slim people."

Jesse requests an apple box and they do not have one. The problem gets solved when Anna reminds her that the camera should be on the floor level.

"Anyway, so you were telling me . . ."

"Yeah, this is for a U.S. tour, it's called Another Stage."

Jesse seems to be very familiar with this theater company. "Another Stage! I have four friends in New York applying for that same tour. It's very selective . . ."

"Like, pushy people are applying for that? Damn, I'm not gonna get anything . . ."

"Oh, no, you might, you might, you just might." Jesse checks the viewfinder again, "OK that looks great."

Anna has to tell her why she always has Bill or

now her to videotape the monologue. "I've a problem with my English you know. Could you like pay attention to what I say?"

"Just be spontaneous . . ."

"That I am!"

"As long as we understand . . . your accent," points out Jesse.

"I am more concerned with the grammar," Anna says.

"No, we like your accent, we like your accent," Jesse reassures her.

"If the joke doesn't come across they don't get it and they don't laugh . . ." Anna starts getting preoccupied.

"We'll get it, we'll get it."

That is the beauty about positive attitudes. Anna tends to notice only what goes wrong or what might go wrong in a given moment or in the far future. Jesse and North American people Anna has met see only the positive at the present time.

Suddenly, Jesse asks a reasonable and an innocent question. "Have you ever thought of opening in Barcelona?"

Anna does not know what to say. Finally she starts mumbling. "Well, Catalan people . . . I don't think they like this kind of thing."

"No, they will, they will. You know I've heard that there is a lot of public money for theater in Barcelona."

"Could you give me that information?"

That really hits home. Anna thinks that maybe she could open someday in Barcelona. Anna tells herself that she has to keep an open mind. When it is good, it is good, here and everywhere. If she is not liked in Barcelona it is because she still has things to polish. Once she does the polishing job, she says to herself, then Barcelona audiences will laugh with her lines just as much as Americans do!

Jesse keeps talking about grants for theater projects. "There's a lot of money available for new people, new artists doing theater in Barcelona, there's a lot of money. I'll give you some applications, just remind me at the end . . . OK?"

Anna Jr. has been standing to the right and to the left of the camera several times while checking the cue cards. Anna and Jesse decide to make her change once again.

The scenery is ready. All men's underwear, lingerie, bright towels, and blankets are displayed and hanging from the lines. The four towers of the Sagrada Familia are again almost hidden by these clothes. Jesse places the camera at the floor level and Anna Jr. stands at her right. The videotaping starts.

Anna feels particularly confident when she gets to one of her favorite parts. The housewife just finishes collecting the clothes which she has put in a bucket. She, as usual, addresses herself straight to the camera. "You know I'm from Valencia but she — my neighbor — she's from Barcelona. She's very cold, very Catalan you know. She's some kind of executive, financial adviser to the Mayor or something like that. I thought lesbians were only in sports . . . Jesus, and in show business. They're everywhere!"

As she pronounces the "l" word, she exits hurriedly — and somehow excited — as if pursued by a wild bunch of women.

The videotaping continues. The open air Mass certainly handicaps the taping of the monologue as

13

far as sound is concerned. The church hymns produce a noteworthy contrast with the content of Anna's monologue and that does not escape Anna. That is why when Jesse warns Anna about the poor sound of some of the takes, Anna indicates that it is OK and that they should go ahead. Anna feels at ease. She performs all the amazing changes the housewife goes through. These intimate changes are underlined by her costumes which eventually are more free and less stiff. At the end, Jesse takes the original tape with her to make copies for Anna.

Anna has high hopes that Another Stage will take her on the tour. This thought keeps her going. She wants to be a playwright. The tour guide job is just to pay the bills.

Once the copies of the video are finished, Anna keeps one at home with her while she puts the other one inside a stuffed envelope and mails it to Another Stage. Along with the NTSC videotape of the monologue, Anna encloses a filled entry form and two copies of the monologue with flashy red covers. Anna has never been to San Francisco. Her acceptance in the U.S. tour is becoming her newest obsession. "I hope they like the videotape in San Francisco. If they want me for the U.S. tour, I'll go around America performing my monologue. Gosh!"

Since she sees that one coming, the obsession, she goes to church. She knows of the great results of meditation because she has read about it. Actually, she likes to go to church to listen to the sermon, especially when the priest has a brilliant day.

Today is not the best day to go to listen to a good sermon. There are a couple of women behind Anna who have decided to pray the rosary right when the priest gets to the good part of the sermon. Anna is really upset. She knows that she has to be tolerant even if they mumble straight in her ears, or even when one of them coughs on the back of Anna's neck.

She has come to the church to fight her new obsession and to listen to the priest. She notices an incredibly beautiful stained glass window. It depicts Martha, the busy sister of more contemplative Maria. Both sisters were great friends of Jesus, as Anna gets the story. All of a sudden, the priest's words shock Anna. He is talking about *Love Thy Neighbor*. Anna's heart pounds.

"*Love Thy Neighbor*, yes sir. That's the title of my monologue!" she thinks.

What a coincidence! Except that she does not believe in coincidences and she takes it as a sign. Coincidences, as far as Anna is concerned, are acts that God does not want to sign. She is absolutely thrilled.

One of the two women behind coughs more strongly. All of a sudden, Anna sees herself propelled to the reclinator. "Damn!"

Once she is out in the open air, Anna makes an important decision. "I'll also try to open the monologue in Barcelona. There's so much public money for theater projects! Oh, what I'll do is I'll pick up all the application forms on my lunch hour."

In fact, with or without high heels she goes like crazy to all the various cultural institutions that grant money for theater projects. Some of these institutions are based in Barcelona, the others have their headquarters in Madrid or Brussels, the capital of the European Economic Market. Some regulations are in Catalan, others in Spanish, and some in French. She picks up all the entry forms, all the guidelines, all the legislation about grants and fund raising tips for theater projects. There are a lot of things to be done and she is hopeful.

In the middle of her particular tour to all the institutions, Anna has a brief moment of self-doubt. As she picks up the regulations for one particular grant, she gets the feeling that she just has the wrong look. She looks at all the other young people in line. They look "right." They also look as if they are nuts. That is how "people from the arts" are supposed to look, though. They wear stuff that nobody else in their right mind would wear. Anna, she looks like a plane Jane. As she stands up there in her blue uniform, she realizes that one of them was wrong, either she or the guys in line.

Later on, when her lunch break is almost over, she has time for another observation. As she sits down to organize all the documents she has collected, she reads all the names of the people at the selection committees. Anna notices one particular name, Miguel Gasòliba. He is on all the selection committees. This is, though, a very Catalan thing. In a small country such as Catalonia, there is a shortage of interesting jobs while an excess of talented people. What generally happens is that one person ends up filling absolutely all the few positions available, and so one can find a "Miguel Gasòliba" in practically every line of business. That is why these people are nicknamed "gods," because they are everywhere.

16

Anna makes all of these considerations and tries to remember where she has heard the name of Miguel Gasòliba before when something unexpected suddenly happens.

She is on her way home with an incredible amount of documents in her hands. Her mind races at top speed about all the things that need to be done regarding her fund raising efforts. She is about to pass by the Sant Andreu Teatre where Marta L. Puig stars in *Oedipus Queen*.

Outside the theater a radio reporter stands by her mobile unit installed in a car. She desperately asks her colleagues at the studio to go on air. Suddenly, Anna understands why the reporter wants to go on air this minute.

Behind the semi-opened theater doors, Marta L. Puig herself discusses a pressing matter with one of her assistants. Marta L. Puig is a woman in her early forties with very short and sophisticated hair. She wears sunglasses. Marta L. Puig has a tremendously expressive face. She is not very tall and looks like she is in very good shape. Her assistant notices the radio reporter and lets Marta L. Puig go.

Anna gets petrified when she recognizes Marta and without planning it, her documents, bag, and umbrella fall on the ground. "Oh no! Marta L. Puig, the Diva of Independent Catalan Theater, and the ex-love of my life . . . I'll never have an affair with an actress again."

The Diva advances toward the tense radio reporter just like a lion toward one of his victims. Walking slowly and with a mischievous smile on her lips, the Diva gets ready for one more of her exhausting duties, the interviews.

Marta L. Puig was Anna's last obsession. Anna is well aware of how destructive that obsession was and since then Anna tries to stay away from any obsession of any kind. Anna keeps telling herself "I'll never have an affair with an actress, nor with anybody who speaks in front of an audience, like . . . like lawyers, priests, politicians . . . teachers!"

Chapter 3

The faculty of engineering in Barcelona has a new professor of Mechanics named Montserrat Ehrzman Rosas. She started working at the school three months ago. She is a smart, sweet, and shy young woman born twenty-seven years ago in Tel Aviv, Israel, and raised in Boston. Montserrat is mild-mannered and does not socialize much. Deep down, she is more interested in her research projects than in her teaching job, but she is resigned at the present time. She used to be a seismic analysis researcher and now she teaches mechanics.

Montserrat tries to get by as well as she can in the faculty of engineering with a particularly talkative dean who is kind of a busy body and what's worst, a friend of Montserrat's uncle. She also has to deal with a colleague of hers, Jordi. He is a nice Catalan boy but too pushy for Montserrat's taste. He always asks her out. Carme Coll is a woman colleague. Carme also teaches mechanics. She is older than Montserrat and she does everything she can to make Montserrat feel at home.

Montserrat has a red Opel car that she parks in the professor's area. Her car key holder has the flag of Israel. On one side of the windshield Montserrat notices a piece of blue flier. It is a flier of Costa Brava Tours. In fact, Anna Jr. has recently been working intensively in the area.

By the Barcelona Football Club Stadium there is the Pink Pavilion, a gorgeous turn of the century pavilion that today is used as a dormitory for students and professors. Montserrat arrives at the parking area of the Pink Pavilion. She has not had time to look for an apartment yet, so she stays at the school's dormitory. Her modest salary makes her accept this affordable housing for the time being. The place looks gorgeous outside, just like an American campus. Montserrat is not very fond of it because her room is very small.

She occupies room 6-C. On her bulletin board she has a Tel Aviv ID card and an invitation for the reception given when the Dean presented her to the rest of the faculty members. She also has several pictures. One picture is of Montserrat with a boyfriend. The other is a close-up of a beautiful woman who has the attractiveness of a Mediterranean classical beauty. Montserrat hangs the Costa Brava Tours leaflet by the woman's photo.

After class, she feels really out of place. She does have papers to grade and classes to prepare, but she feels sad, utterly bored, and alone. Montserrat picks up the phone and calls the front desk. "Hi, this is Montserrat Ehrzman Rosas from room 6-C. Could you recommend to me any tour, any guided tour? Thank you." She hangs up.

Montserrat looks at the blue flier. She never heard of the Costa Brava before. Would she be so bored as to take a guided tour? She decides to sleep on it.

Completely awake and at full blast, Anna summons her tourists at Gaudí Avenue. Behind her hangs an advertisement of the successful play *Oedipus Queen*, Marta L. Puig's latest show.

Anna has the faxed list of names in her hands, and she wears her blue uniform and her white blouse. She seems to have overcome yesterday's shock when she encountered the ex-love of her life. At the present time, a French tourist keeps her busy.

"May I suggest that you cover a little bit the teets . . . *oui la poitrine s'il vous plaît, on va se refroidir s'il y a de la Tramontane*" [If the Tramuntana wind blows, you can get a real nice cold], Anna warns her. The tour guide is ready to check all the names on her list. Anna goes straight for the first name on the list and reads it out loud.

"Montserrat Ehrzman Rosas . . . are you from Israel?"

Montserrat produces a forced smile and nods. That is not all, though. Anna always tries to make tourists feel at home. She uses the few words she might know in 13 languages every time she can.

"*Evenuh Shalom alehem, evenuh Shalom, Shalom alehem. Oi bei.* Who is next?"

Fifteen minutes later Anna has managed to get everybody on the bus. Some of the tourists have already started the videotaping session. Coincidentally, Anna takes a seat by the Israeli young woman. Not many seats are free. Anna notices that Montserrat looks like a real New Yorker, but without the lifeless white skin. The trip to Costa Brava has just started. In an hour they will be in the middle of wilderness, at some wooden beaches.

Anna has shocked herself. She never pays attention to physical features but she finds the eyes of Montserrat Ehrzman Rosas absolutely remarkable. The truth is that Anna feels Montserrat's eyes are nothing extraordinary until she smiles. When Montserrat smiles, those eyes are no longer eyes. They become a couple of guns shooting at you, and you are dead. Again, she never pays attention to anybody's physical features.

Anna perceives another deadly weapon in Montserrat . . . her white perfect teeth. They have the capacity of drawing the most charming smile. She just kills you without being aware of that because on the surface, Montserrat looks perfectly shy. To make things even more explosive she has what Anna considers an irresistible contralto voice. At this point, half an hour away from Barcelona, they each tell the other the story of her life.

"I was born in Tel Aviv," Montserrat tells Anna

with her velvet voice, "and then at seven my parents moved to Boston and I was raised in Boston, but I lived in New York for a short while as well."

"Where in New York?" asks Anna, really excited.

They start talking about New York City. Anna remembers Columbia Bagels, at 110th and Broadway, the best bagel store in the world. Montserrat agrees with her on that point. Montserrat confesses that she loves bagels as much as Anna does. Anna mentions to Montserrat that since she is Jewish, she should visit the Medieval Jewish ghetto in Girona, a city an hour's drive from Barcelona and near the Costa Brava. Anna spells "Girona" for her.

"Montserrat" is a very Catalan name, not very well known abroad. Anna explains to Montserrat how surprised she was when she noticed a Lillian Hellman play titled "Montserrat." What certainly shocks Anna even more is to meet an Israeli woman named Montserrat. Again with her velvet voice, Montserrat explains the reason.

"My grandparents fled the Nazis and they stayed at the monastery in Montserrat, and they thought it was a great name and they gave it to me."

The highway runs parallel to vineyards. A sign on the highway shows they are getting closer to Costa Brava. The sign also gives information about the different activities one can do at the Costa Brava: taking photographs, camping, and sun tanning.

Anna realizes that she forgot, almost completely, the rest of the group. Anna goes by the driver and takes the mike to warn people about the very strong Tramuntana wind, a furious Catalan wind. Anna is happy to have met such an interesting tourist. Montserrat travels alone and she must feel lonely.

Suddenly Anna decides to invite everybody who knows the "Evenuh Shalom" song to join in for a forgettable rendition of this Jewish folk song.

The irony is that everybody who, like Anna, has been a member of the Catholic Girl Scouts movement knows that song by heart. It is listed in the Girl Scout Traditional Popular Songs booklet. During the Catholic Mass, the same melody is often sung with Catalan lyrics.

Unfortunately, the singing gives Montserrat a terrible headache. The fact is that once they arrive at Palamós, a village in the Costa Brava, Montserrat looks quite groggy. Anna comes out of the bus and Montserrat stops her.

"Anna" (that is the first time Anna has heard Montserrat pronouncing her name in her contralto voice), "do you know where I can buy an aspirin?"

"An aspirin? What's wrong?"

"Just a headache. I'll take it easy though."

"Well I have some. Why don't you ... they are here in this bag, OK?" Anna babbles and suddenly, she hands her big bag over to Montserrat. "Could you hold that for me?"

"Sure."

"There's some reading material here, so if you feel bored, feel free, OK? Montserrat, I hope you feel better."

Anna leaves.

Anna is not aware of what she has just said to Montserrat. All she knows is that Montserrat's presence does not leave her indifferent, and that she cannot help noticing Montserrat's cute eyes, her beautiful smile and her contralto voice.

On the other hand, Anna wants to hide her

disappointment. She does not like Montserrat staying away from the group. Anna wants all along not to show her real feelings.

Montserrat stays at the deserted beach on the sand by the sea. The group starts their excursion. Anna's red umbrella is always with her, as she leads the group toward the top of a mountain from which they will see a gorgeous view of Platja Castell. At the top of the mountain there are the ruins of an Iberic town.

The special beauty about the Catalan Costa Brava is the mixture of the transparent blue of the sea with the green from the pine trees. It is almost as if woody pine tree forests would enter the Mediterranean sea. Some parts of the Coast are rocky and the beaches are very small, like baby bays, then they are not called beaches, they are called *Cales*. An American tourist once told Anna that Costa Brava is like the beaches at Carmel, northern California, except that you can take a nice swim in the Costa Brava and it is less agreeable to do it in northern California.

All of a sudden Anna freaks out. She knew she was doing something wrong when handing her bag over to Montserrat, but she could not help it. She had to keep talking to hide her disappointment. Now she realizes what she has done. Inside her big bag there is the final version of her monologue *Love Thy Neighbor*. What if Montserrat glances at the monologue and reads some of it?

In fact, Montserrat is incredibly bored and she hates herself for having taken a guided tour. She does not feel well at all and she is not seduced by the beauty that surrounds her. The waves do nothing but increase her splitting headache. Almost at her feet, there is a big fisherman's net brought by the waves. It might have belonged to a fisherman's boat.

Montserrat notices a beautiful, tall woman by the sea, probably a tourist. She looks at her. Then she turns her eyes toward the other side of the bay, where a guy jogs. She notices he is in shape. Eventually she sees the big bag Anna has left her. Montserrat cleans the sand from her hands and gets the bag. She opens the zipper.

What she first notices when she opens the bag is the red covers of *Love Thy Neighbor*. She picks it up and lies on the sand. Slowly, she opens it and glances at it.

HOUSEWIFE'S VOICE
"And so I suggested that she might be a lesbian because she was missing some hormones."

At once, Montserrat closes the monologue and sits down. Montserrat hopes that the group will soon be back because it is hot and she has no umbrella to protect her from the sun. Slowly, she looks around and again cleans the sand from her hands. She lies back. Her hands reach for the monologue one more time.

HOUSEWIFE'S VOICE
"To devote yourself to your career and then to the maintenance of your boyfriend, cooking, washing, ironing, unacceptable she told me.

And on top of that you have to listen to them?"

Montserrat thinks of the Dean. He is just like that. How many times has she thought why does she have to listen to his thoughts, to his speeches, to his opinions . . . She started to like this stuff. Then there are some other more intimate parts in the monologue.

HOUSEWIFE
"And then, the way she looked at me, with her green eyes . . . Oh that look. Those eyes seemed to touch me inside."

Those parts made Montserrat think of the woman whose photograph hangs on her bulletin board. Montserrat remembers that beautiful face with classical features. She had a terrific, an unforgettable, look in her eyes as well.

In the meantime, Anna is with all the tourists up on the hill. Her red umbrella shows them her whereabouts at all times. Montserrat can see her too.

"I hated the Costa Brava when I was a kid but then I spent five years in New York City writing roach killer commercials, and then I started to appreciate the Costa Brava."

Anna never objects to answering any personal questions the tourists might ask. She figures that when she becomes a celebrity, she will have to get used to it. If they do not understand what a roach is, she kindly spells the word for them.

"Roach? 'R', 'O', 'A', 'C', 'H' . . ."

They come down from the excursion and Anna still answers questions. "I hate advertising to the point that . . ." Suddenly Anna checks the time. She resumes her philosophy in no time. "Oh, it's lunch time."

Anna comes down to the beach when she observes a pine with its roots on the rock. She admires that. How is it possible for the pine to survive in such tough conditions?

Montserrat sees the group coming back to the bus. She takes with her the fisherman's net. Both women meet by the sea.

"Hi, Montserrat, how are you feeling?"

"Fine, thank you."

Anna notices that Montserrat tries desperately to sound perfectly balanced, just as she herself tried to do when they last spoke.

"Do you really feel better?"

"Good . . . Yeah."

"I"m very glad, I'm very glad."

Montserrat gives Anna back her bag. "Oh here, here is your bag."

"Thank you."

"You're welcome." After a pause, Montserrat asks, "Hey, Anna, can I read your play?"

"My monologue . . ."

"Sorry, your monologue."

"Sure, do you like reading between the lines?" Anna tests Montserrat.

"Excuse me?"

With this as Montserrat's answer, Anna realizes Montserrat did not get it. The question for Anna now is, "is she teachable?"

Before leaving the beach, Montserrat honors one of the activities recommended on the road sign about the Costa Brava. She takes a picture. She does not photograph a person nor does she ask to be photographed at the Costa Brava. She shoots the mountain by Platja Castell where Anna took the group. The color photo will probably join the ones she already has on her board at room 6-C.

When they get back to Barcelona, everybody is tired. As usual, the floor of the bus gets covered with blue fliers. Tourists just want to have a good time, they do not care much about where exactly the Costa Brava is located. For those who care, the flier explains that the Catalan Costa Brava is at the Mediterranean Riviera, the closest cities being Barcelona, Girona, and Marseilles.

The next day, Anna notices that it has taken her twenty-four complete hours to come to the realization that she is a masochist. Here she is invariably at the very same spot of Gaudí Avenue summoning new tourists. This spot has a big advertisement of Marta L. Puig's play *Oedipus Queen*. Why does she keep doing that? she wonders. Today when she faced Marta's big close-up on the poster, she asks herself, "Why?" Maybe because it is pleasurable for her, this kind of suffering? Is that her concept of fun? Anna finally decides to greet the group.

"Are we having fun yet?" she asks the tourists.

Chapter 4

At the school of engineering, Jordi definitely pursues some fun. He encounters Montserrat right before her class and he wants to impress her. In the classroom, an empty bottle hangs from the ceiling. Jordi hits the bottle and goes near Montserrat. He takes out some notes from the pocket of his lab coat. Jordi ceremoniously reads his notes. *"Evenuh Shalom alehem, evenuh Shalom, Shalom alehem."*

Montserrat smiles politely.

After the class, Jordi meets her at the hall, in

front of the elevators. "Every time I ask you out, it always happens to be a Jewish religious day. Why?"

Montserrat shrugs.

In her tiny and crowded room, Montserrat recalls parts of the monologue as she caresses the red covers.

"And then, the way she looked at me, with her green eyes . . . Oh that look. Those eyes seemed to touch me inside."

Montserrat takes a deep breath. The fisherman's net sits beside her. Her hand reaches out for her telephone.

The end of the painting job will suffer a new postponement because today Anna is not in the mood. She is deeply concerned. Maybe she is not all set with a job and a vocation. Maybe she is in need of extracurricular distractions. The problem is the Diva. Anna thought she had the Diva, Marta L. Puig, out of her mind, but maybe she did not. Actually, it is quite difficult to do something like that in a city like Barcelona. Marta L. Puig's face is not only on practically all the walls in the city announcing her play but she is also in the back of magazines, or in every daily newspaper. Anna, resigned, takes a deep breath.

"Marta, Marta, *merda*..."

At this point, the telephone rings. When the outgoing message is over, a somehow familiar voice shocks Anna.

"Anna, this is Montserrat. I'm done with your play. My number is..."

Anna doubts. She thought she had no chance with Montserrat. Probably, she will only want to give the monologue back.

Two hours later they both sit on a bench in front of the University housing where Montserrat lives. Anna ignores why Montserrat did not want to meet inside.

"Thank you for coming," says Montserrat, dressed as an executive. She looks more beautiful than ever. She is radiant.

"Oh, my pleasure," Anna replies wearing the only decent jacket she has.

"I ... your play ... it was fantastic."

"The monologue."

"Oh, I'm sorry, monologue."

"Because, you know I think there's a kind of parallelism between monologue and masturbation. I'm always a little bit embarrassed but I gotta say it's not a play, it's a monologue."

"I felt ... I mean ... the play, I loved it."

"Thank you, I appreciate it."

"You're welcome."

Anna has the feeling that Montserrat is trying to tell her something.

"You know," Montserrat proceeds, "I've always had a terrific relationship with men but..."

"Good for you."

"Thank you. But at the same time, you know

there's always been like a little something missing. Now, don't get me wrong, the men I've been with are quite good but . . ."

"Good," Anna replies without actually caring much.

"Yeah, I like men. I like to have sex with guys. Hummm . . . but at the same time I . . . well . . . kind of . . ." The memory of her beautiful girlfriend crosses Montserrat's mind. She is too shy to verbalize what she needs to say. Plus, she has not been in a situation like that for a long time.

All of a sudden Anna realizes that the dormitory is the Pink Pavilion. "Oh, you know this is the Pink Pavilion? This is the old pavilion for single mothers during the last century in Barcelona. You have a room there?"

"Yeah."

"Oh that's very interesting. I love it. I'm sorry what were you saying about men?"

"Oh. Never mind."

Chapter 5

Gaudí Avenue has the Temple of the Sagrada Familia on one end and the Saint Paul Hospital, an Art Nouveau hospital, on the other. The hospital is a breathtaking architectural ensemble of Catalan Modernism from the beginning of the century. There are practically no visible straight lines; it is all about round forms. Domes of all kinds crown the pavilions. Rich decorations in all possible colors embellish the facades. Anna likes the daring and the originality of it. Each pavilion is different. Gynecology Pavilion, for instance, does not look like Thaumatology Pavilion at all.

Anna and Montserrat have been rambling all over this hospital complex and they are tired. They are also less tense than when they met earlier in the afternoon. They sit on the stairs of one of the hospital pavilions, the one of Gynecology. Anna looks toward the sky. "I think is gonna blow the Tramuntana wind," Anna says, just to break the insidious silence.

"What's the Tramuntana wind?" Montserrat asks.

"Oh, it's a Catalan wind, very strong. You've been in Barcelona now for how long?"

"For three months."

"And are you seeing someone?"

"Well . . . not exactly." Montserrat smiles.

"Huh? Yes or not?"

"There's this one guy at school, Jordi, who seems to be showing some interest."

"Oh, he's Catalan."

"Yes."

"Good. That's wonderful."

"That's OK, not a big deal," points out Montserrat.

At this point Anna cannot tell if Montserrat means that being a Catalan is not a big deal or that going out with a guy is not big deal. Talking to Montserrat is an experience filled with endless suspense. When she is near Montserrat, Anna feels "in the mood." Since Montserrat is so cryptic about herself, there is no way for Anna to know whether she would have any chance.

Fortunately, Montserrat is willing to tell a little

bit more about herself. Anna, who is completely unable to look Montserrat straight in the eyes, does her best in adopting a relatively aloof attitude. Her attention to every word that Montserrat pronounces is total.

"No, I mean," Montserrat starts, "after dating a lot of guys . . . like this one guy I dated for example, if he had the choice between me and a new car, I'm sure he'd pick the new car. I don't know the guys you dated but for me it was always the same story. If they were with me for too long they always had to prove their independence. I got tired of it after a while. Yes . . . I get more out of a relationship with a woman."

Anna's efforts to maintain a poker face fail completely at this point. Montserrat's confession after two hours of conversation leaves Anna utterly dumbfounded. She looks at Montserrat with amazement. Anna's most basic intellectual capacity is seriously diminished, otherwise she would have registered and interpreted the sexy killer look that Montserrat gave her.

Once she has started, Montserrat decides to tell it all. Anna is all ears. "I went out with a woman several years ago, the relationship lasted two years . . ."

"How old are you now, Montserrat?"

"Twenty-seven." Montserrat looks much younger. "It was my first relationship with a woman and after that I dated a lot of guys. I never . . . we broke up because she got married. It was so painful when we broke up that ever since then I avoided falling into relationships like that again."

Anna does register the "falling into." At this point Anna would like to stand up and leave. There is nothing to do as far as she is concerned. On the other hand, Anna has always admired mature women, people who know what they are doing, what they want, women who have gone through a lot, even designing women. However, she has never "fallen" for bimbos yet to be taught about the basics.

Montserrat is not too concerned about Anna's silence. Montserrat actually devotes all her energies to summon the courage she needs to ask Anna "the" question. Anna is an experienced woman. Montserrat thinks she will never have an opportunity like this again. She just has to ask her.

"May I ask you a question?" Montserrat suddenly asks.

"Yes." Anna suspects it might be something interesting.

"OK. When did you know you were a lesbian?" Montserrat blurts out.

"People don't generally label me a lesbian, they label me nuts. When I tell them that I've been in love with a woman for five years and that I went to bed with her only twice, they don't consider me a lesbian, they consider me nuts. She was in show business and . . ." Montserrat listens to Anna with complete abandon. On the other hand Anna fears that if the poor woman asks her next whether "you're born . . . or you become . . ." she won't be able to control herself.

Fortunately, instead of asking further about Anna, Montserrat prefers to state clearly what her feelings or fears are. "I'm scared to think of having a relationship with another woman. Once . . . no, once was enough, too painful. No matter how much I sometimes . . . No . . . No way."

37

Anna has had it. Her response is immediate. "Well but Montserrat, in life you've got to be brave. Otherwise, look, you're not doing men, you're not doing women . . . you'll be doing a lot of museums."

Chapter 6

Park Güell, built at the beginning of this century by Antoni Gaudí, is Barcelona's most magical place, and that is exactly where the group heads up to as Anna gets ready to start a new tour.

"OK, let's hit it!" They all jump at the bus.

Antoni Gaudí had a very rich sponsor, and that person was Count Güell. Gaudí planned a quite artistic urban development in Barcelona in a completely revolutionary way. All the houses were different from one another. A central market, sculptures, fountains and parks surrounded the few houses. The inspiration was always in nature: caves, caverns. The texture of its designs, the apparent simplicity, the imaginative shapes are the work of an extraordinary creative mind. That is why Gaudí is considered a genius with a great command not only in architecture but in decoration and sculpting.

Park Güell looks like surreal or fairy tale scenery for some. Japanese tourists absolutely adore this style. Gaudí would go in person to Valencia tile factories and buy broken parts. With these broken parts, he would make collages that now embellish the surfaces of benches and sculptures. It is said that Gaudí was a very bad-tempered person. He insisted on supervising almost everything when not doing it himself — from the clay models to wrought-iron — and consequently he drove workers crazy. Mr. Güell went bankrupt before Gaudí finished his job. Park Güell could not get finished.

Following Anna's red umbrella, the tourists see it all: the dragon fountain at the entry, the wrought-iron, the circular benches, and the baroque iron doors of some of the entries.

Park Güell is the best place for Anna to be today. There are no pay phones. She would like to call Montserrat but she is reluctant to. She feels she should not call her because she is always too impulsive. The desire to call her is so strong. On the other hand, deep down she hates falling for somebody. When she falls in love with a person, she obsesses over her and this is not productive. It is a distraction. Then Anna remembers Montserrat's velvet voice and, "Will she be thinking about me today," Anna wonders.

In fact, Montserrat is thinking about Anna. She is

at the mechanics lab and she smiles. She remembers what Anna said to the French lady about her "teets." Today Montserrat does not regret having taken the tour.

Anna remembers Montserrat and the lengthy conversation they had before going to the Costa Brava. Anna admits that Montserrat opened up her heart to her. It must not have been easy for the woman to tell it all to an almost complete stranger.

Montserrat makes an effort and tries to regain concentration on her work. Meanwhile, Anna stands by a telephone booth. Her urge to call is overwhelming. She is about to enter the booth, but she finally leaves.

Back home, there are no messages on Anna's machine. Anna is aware that she should finish painting the apartment but before that, she must listen just once more to the message Montserrat left yesterday. "I'm done with your play . . ." Anna listens to the message over and over again.

In the meantime, Montserrat exits the faculty main building and she enters a pay phone booth. She takes out of her lab coat a piece of paper and dials Anna's number. It is busy.

Anna goes out for a walk. Montserrat does not have all the time in the world to make phone calls since she has to follow her class schedule. When Anna is back she has some messages on her machine. Her heart pounds as she listens to them.

Montserrat tries again. She enters the telephone booth and dials Anna's number. It is busy again.

Anna has finished checking her machine and there is no message from Montserrat. Anna definitely thinks that there is nothing more to do with her.

Montserrat sits in her room grading papers. Suddenly, she breaks off, as her mind wanders. Her production levels temporarily decrease, just like Anna's, but she takes it with a smile. She looks up at her Costa Brava Tours flier. Anna's phone number is written with a red ink pen.

At night, Anna's telephone ringing sounds like a bomb. She immediately picks it up.

"*Digueu* [Hello]?"

"Anna, it's Montserrat."

"Hi," is all Anna can say.

"I . . . just . . . I just had a crazy idea."

"Hmmmm. Generally they are the best ones, shoot."

"OK . . . would you like to go to the Costa Brava this weekend?"

"To the Costa Brava?" Anna is shocked.

"To the Costa Brava," Montserrat's velvet voice concedes.

The painting job will be postponed until next weekend.

Chapter 7

Montserrat parks her red Opel Corsa under the pine trees at Cala S'Alguer. The fishermen's small houses are nearby. Anna and Montserrat make their way toward Platja Castell walking on roads paved with pine needles and surrounded by green pine trees. The intense Mediterranean scent of rosemary, pine, and thyme along with the furious waters of the Mediterranean sea that give the name to the Catalan Costa Brava seduce Montserrat. It is colder than Montserrat thought it would be. She is not wearing a jacket.

On their way to the Iberic ruins, Montserrat takes some pictures. The Bay of Platja Castell can be seen from the top of the mountain. Montserrat regrets now not having joined the group the first time she arrived at the Costa Brava. All she did was take a color picture of the mountain. She does love what she sees. The green and the blue mix in the Costa Brava in every possible manner. It is a gorgeous spectacle.

Montserrat takes a seat on a safe rock by the mountain while Anna likes to get closer to the cliff. The brave waters look wild today. She cannot miss it. Eventually, Anna goes toward Montserrat and takes her to a higher place, with yet a better view and less wind.

Facing Cala S'Alguer, they can see the car parked far away. They find a small pine tree to protect them from the wind and they sit by it. When the incomparable beauty of nature has filled their spirits, they occupy themselves with more earthy urges.

"I mean it's not on the looks or anything like that. Well, intelligence is important to me, somebody who can make me laugh...tall, tall, I like tall women." Montserrat discloses to Anna this kind of personal information about herself. By now Anna knows that Montserrat can feel attracted to women. The only question mark in Anna's mind is whether Montserrat likes her or not. Anna wonders how much longer she will have to wait to find out.

It is windy and getting colder. Montserrat trembles and Anna notices it.

"Are you OK?" Anna asks Montserrat.

"Yeah."

"You're shaking!"

"No, I'm fine."

"Montserrat, you're trembling . . . it's chilly."

"It's a little bit cold, but it's nice up here."

Anna puts her arm around Montserrat, in a protective move. Anna feels obliged to do so if only because she is bigger than Montserrat. "Come over here. Don't be so structured. You're trembling!"

"No, I'm not, it's my heart pounding." Montserrat is having fun.

"Yeah, for Jordi, right? Look, how do you call that in English?"

"Skin."

"No, the *goose pimpoodles*."

"Yeah, the *goose pimpoodles*, it's perfect . . ."

"Don't make fun . . ."

It turns colder and they move to another spot. In this area a part of the rocky mountain is completely perforated. It is like a cave. In the summer, small boats have great fun as they enter through one end and appear again through the other.

"What are you going to show me?" Montserrat asks.

"Oh, nothing spectacular really, my meditation spot."

"Really?"

"Yeah, it's good. It sort of puts your life into perspective."

"God, I need that."

It is great that Anna does not have vertigo because her meditation spot is right at the top of a precipice. The green waters reflect the color of the trees. Montserrat prefers a safer place by the sea. Anna cannot meditate. She knows how good it is to do it but she cannot, at least not now. Anna just thinks about Montserrat. "Tall, tall, I like tall women," that is what she said. Anna does not know how to take it. Montserrat smiles at her whenever they cross glances. Anna thinks "The cramps in my belly are killing me. I'll have to make the first move. I hate that."

They are about to go back to Platja Castell. Anna goes by a tree she likes very dearly. It is windy and she grabs one of the branches and thinks to herself, "OK here we go. I'm going to make the first move."

"I love this Tramuntana wind. Montserrat, I'm older than you are ..."

"And taller," Montserrat replies quite amused.

"And I'm going to give you a kiss, may I?"

"Please."

"Good."

As Anna goes nearer to Montserrat, she remembers a crucial concept in life, and in drama. "Oh, simplicity, it always works."

They enter the red Opel Corsa parked at Cala S'Alguer by the small deserted fishermen's houses. The idea was just to kiss but one thing led to another and it took them an hour and thirty minutes to leave the car.

Apparently the women who exit the Opel Corsa are the same ones that entered the car ninety minutes earlier. Except now all the cards are on the table and facing up. When Anna exits the car she mumbles without finding the right words to say. She can barely stand up for her legs do not feel firm. She tries to put her sunglasses on but her hands still tremble. Anna was the one who supposedly was leading the way, but she cannot tell at this point where to go, nor what to do.

On the other side of the car, from the driver's

side, a serene and balanced Montserrat got out. She takes her time savoring the moment and leans toward the car as she watches Anna coming out of it. First she gives Anna a compulsory look, then she starts to smile, slowly. She puts her sunglasses on with determination and she leads the way toward the fishermen's houses. Anna follows her.

As the sun sets, they look at Platja Castell again from the top of the mountain. Anna feels like she is in heaven and she wishes she could die. She thinks she will never feel as happy as she does right now.

Montserrat wonders how much the same locations change depending on one's feelings. She does not want to think much about anything at this moment, especially not about the fact that she is again involved with a woman. Right now all that counts to her is that with the gorgeous Platja Castell at her feet and Anna by her side, there is not a more beautiful place in the world to be than the Costa Brava. Montserrat takes a last picture of the Costa Brava, this time of the fishermen's houses.

Chapter 8

Anna loves it when Montserrat enjoys the sites in Barcelona that she herself adores. They ramble around Saint Paul's Hospital. Anna is amazed when she catches herself listening to Montserrat. It is a terrific experience for Anna to stop thinking about her problems and start paying attention to somebody else's. Montserrat is not very happy with her work situation.

"I hate teaching. I mean I can't show it in front of the kids but I hate . . . I don't like it." They stroll around the hospital garden as she continues. "It's not

the teaching part I don't like so much, it's just . . .
when I came to this job they promised me some
research, a couple of classes a week and research and
it ends up I'm teaching six courses a week. I feel so
frustrated. I don't mind teaching. I've done it before.
I did it in Boston, I did it for a while in New York
but I don't want to be a teacher, I want to be a
researcher and this is so frustrating."

Anna's mind flies at once trying to think of a
solution. What could she do for her? Montserrat
continues. "You know the part I hate the most? The
administration . . . the bureaucracy . . . who needs it? I
just wanna get in there and teach my classes. I don't
wanna go to faculty meetings, I don't wanna go to
deans' parties. I would like to teach, get out of there
at the end of the day, research, I would like some
usage of the facilities but this politics of who's there,
who has seniority, who has access to the facilities,
it's nonsense. And you know, I bet I get treated
differently because I'm a woman. In fact, I'm sure of
it. The Dean . . . just because he knows my uncle, he
thinks he can bargain on me anytime and treat me
like I am his niece. I'm not his niece. I'm sorry . . . I
just get so frustrated . . . thanks for letting me get
that off my chest. I'm sorry."

Anna believes in change. Sooner or later, you get
the chance to change what you do not like in your
life and when that opportunity comes, you had better
be ready. That is her philosophy. Anna is not a fan
of resignation.

As in the Costa Brava, there are pine trees also
in this hospital area. Every time Anna sees pine
needles on the ground, she remembers that weekend
at the Catalan coast with Montserrat.

Sometimes Anna spends hours at room 6-C with Montserrat. Anna is amazed at how much homework a professor has. Montserrat always has papers to grade. Anna thinks that Montserrat has a superior IQ, and one day she even measured Montserrat's head with a measuring tape.

When Anna works as a tour guide and suddenly she thinks of Montserrat, she is glad to know that her life now is not just about work and rehearsals, rehearsals and work. The couple is up on a pink cloud. That is also the reason why no progress has been done on her apartment painting job. That is a problem because tonight Montserrat is staying over. "That must be the reason why I feel so happy. I hope she likes the violin I bought for her," Anna thinks to herself.

The smell of paint is still there a few hours later but the place looks nice. They sit on the living room sofa while Montserrat struggles with a bottle of *cava*, the Catalan version of French Champagne. Montserrat bought a cake that Anna studies carefully while also keeping an eye on the bottle of *cava*.

"This is low-cal cake?" Anna is interested to know.

"Low calorie, diet cake," Montserrat answers.

"Oh." Anna hands over a present, "Happy third month anniversary."

The box contains a small violin. "Oh, sweetheart, thank you. It's so nice."

"My great-grandmother used to say something about women and violins," Anna points out.

"What was that?"

"I don't remember."

"Oh well." She looks back at the bottle of *cava*. "Okay." Montserrat has decided to open the bottle.

"I feel romantic this evening."

"Mmmmmm . . . good day yesterday?" Montserrat inquires.

Anna grabs a cushion and hugs it. "No, I think it's something I had for lunch but I would like to do some *bubu cuchi frito rock and roll please baby please* . . ."

"You wanna make love?"

When that velvet sensual voice of Montserrat's pronounces this sentence, Anna freaks out.

"You wanna make love?" Montserrat repeats.

"Yes."

"OK."

"Yes, but only for half an hour because tomorrow I have to wake up real early and go to the Costa Brava."

"OK. That'll be enough time."

"Just kidding, we'll have forty-five minutes."

"What? Did you have dessert too?" Montserrat asks. "OK Anna, you know, I think I'm gonna start writing monologues."

"Monologues!" Anna panics. What is the matter with their relationship, sex relationship that is?

Montserrat, all of a sudden, makes the mistake of pointing at Anna with the bottle. "Anyway can you help me with this?" In doing that, Montserrat scares the hell out of Anna.

"Damn! Oh my God!"

Montserrat does not understand. "What?"

"My libido! It's under zero now." The

psychological impact caused by the bottle pointing at Anna did it. It is something she never mentioned to a professional mental health worker but Champagne bottles scare her when about to be opened. "It scared me to death this thing . . . don't do that, you see what you've done? I was . . . ready for it. I was ready for it! Now I'm cold like a fish!"

Montserrat likes Anna's clowning. The engineering instructor is the best thing that ever happened to Anna. The cake gets finally lit with three candles. Eventually, the bottle gets opened also.

Chapter 9

They spend all the time they can together, that is why the pink cloud is all around. When Montserrat does not have to teach a class, she joins Anna for a break at Gaudí Avenue. Anna cannot believe what she feels. "I'm so happy, I feel like a zombie. I haven't even thought about the monologue for two days now."

The housewife comes back to Anna's mind as they wait for an answer from the selection committee of Another Stage in San Francisco. It was a good idea that the housewife always talked straight to the camera. If Anna gets in the U.S. tour, she will have to face the audience anyway. Anna remembers that when she videotaped the monologue up there on the rooftop, the Mass in the open air was to celebrate the international year of the family. Anna tried to adapt this event into the monologue. The housewife, as usual, kept talking straight to the camera while folding a towel.

"Do you hear all that noise? That's the catholic family reunion — Christians — but at her house, the *lesbian's* house ... very quiet, no orgies, no scandals ... no tennis players ... quiet."

That was the part of the monologue where the housewife has already taken a thorough look at her bachelor neighbor. To her surprise, the neighbor is quite elegant, nothing like she expected.

"She's very smart, wears perfume ... nice nails, I mean nice."

She is very assertive when coming to this area of expertise of hers ... fingernails.

Anna remembers this part of the monologue while Montserrat discloses episodes of her past to Anna. Every now and then, Anna makes new discoveries about Montserrat. It seems reading the monologue had aroused Montserrat. Anna feels completely in another world since she met Montserrat.

"I don't even know what day it is today." Anna wonders, "Am I supposed to work today? Oh yes."

Anna must gather at once the tourists who are

going to take the city tour. She goes to her usual spot to meet the group. She already checked with the company and the location of the meeting point with the tourists cannot be changed. With her back to Marta's poster, she checks the names gotten through fax.

"Are you all ready for your close-ups here? OK, fine." Anna always throws this line to amuse any gay person within the tourists. If there are any, she figures that they will recognize at once that line from *Sunset Boulevard*. She always survives the tour much better if there are openly gay persons among the tourists.

Nobody ever told Anna that the tour had to have a precise duration. Every time she knows that Montserrat waits for her at Gaudí Avenue, the tour becomes much shorter. "More intense," as she puts it.

If there is a majority of Japanese tourists, she knows she cannot avoid the two main Gaudí buildings at the Passeig de Gracia. One of them is Casa Batlló, with its surreal facade decorated with sea motifs, and the roof imitating the skin of a pre-diluvian animal. The other Antoni Gaudí building is Casa Mila, a building that raised controversy when built. They accused Gaudí of literally transporting some caves to Barcelona's most fashionable boulevard.

After the tour, Anna always asks if they have any questions. When Montserrat waits for her, she still asks the same question except that she seems to forget to give the tourists enough time for any question to be posed.

* * * * *

They are in a phase in their relationship where everyday they discover something new about each other. Recently they were in the car and Montserrat was setting up her automatic camera so that both of them could be in the picture. She was shooting black and white. Anna finds Montserrat wonderful and thinks she makes the most amazing comments. She is also shocked by some of these comments, like the one shouted at her right before they had the black and white photo taken. "I'm not a lesbian, OK? Just because I like to sleep with you."

Anna was in a state of shock. At first she wondered if this comment projected an attitude in Montserrat that eventually would put their relationship in jeopardy in the long run. Later, she considered that the relationship could suffer from it in the short run. Finally, Anna decided to stop thinking about it.

Tonight after work, Anna wants to show Montserrat a very beautiful part of Barcelona. It is called Montjuich which in old Catalan language means Jewish Mountain. A Jewish cemetery is in that part of the city, and that is where the name comes from. At night, hundreds of water fountains in the main avenue are lit. From the top of the National Palace, blue rays cross the sky. It is really spectacular. The whole complex was built for the 1898 International Exposition.

They both walk around Montjuich. Anna carries her red umbrella with her and watches Montserrat. "Montserrat can be so American sometimes. She is wearing her lab coat now, because she feels cold.

Practical." Anna finds American people to be very practical.

All of a sudden, Anna notices two women having an argument. It is definitely a lover's quarrel. They look great — like models. Montserrat pays special attention to them but Anna does not realize this. Anna is very soon distracted by a radio reporter — the same reporter she saw that day in front of Saint Andreu Theater trying to interview Marta L. Puig. The poor woman now tries to get on the air but she cannot. She never gets the chance to be on the air. She insists to go on the air because her interviewee waits by her.

Anna turns pale when she catches the interviewee's name. "Did she say Miguel Gasòliba? I must get his business card. That's the guy who's on all the selection committees that grant money for theater projects," Anna thinks. Anna leaves Montserrat for a moment holding the red umbrella. She goes straight to Miguel Gasòliba and the radio interviewer. He is very charming. He is a middle aged man with long hair that reminds her of Beethoven's hair. He does not look like a bureaucrat but rather like a born artist. He gives Anna his business card, putting all of his books on top of the radio reporter's notes. The reporter is almost off balance. That was a very good contact.

Back with Montserrat, they walk toward the National Palace while Montserrat is still mysteriously taken by these women. Montserrat has been observing them closely while she was by herself. So closely, in fact, that one of the women felt upset by

Montserrat's intriguing look. Definitely Montserrat has something on her mind.

Back at her room, Montserrat keeps thinking that she should confront Anna and have a straight talk with her. Different ideas come to Montserrat's mind as to what needs to be said and clarified once and for all. "This is not going to work, Anna. I'm not a lesbian. A relationship between two women is not socially acceptable, it wasn't then and it isn't now. I'm not a lesbian, but I like to sleep with you." She repeats it to herself over and over.

"But how to start the conversation?" she wonders. Maybe with an honest, "Listen, this is not going to work, Anna."

With Miguel Gasòliba's card in her hands, Anna's fund raising gets a new impulse. Anna spends her entire Saturday morning filling out grant applications, xeroxing press clips, filling out more applications, ordering dubs of the photographs, writing memos, resumes, work schedules . . . xeroxing it all, translating the same information into different languages and more xeroxing . . . She wonders, "I have to go through all that for my opening in Barcelona? I hate fund raising."

Fortunately, the telephone rings. It is Montserrat and Anna can tell by her tone that something is wrong.

"Hi. No, no. It's nothing. But we have to talk. Yes, now." Montserrat says.

Anna freaks out and rushes out the door.

They meet at Gaudí Avenue, with the Temple of

the Sagrada Familia behind them. Montserrat is already there when Anna arrives. Anna clowns when passing by Montserrat. She acts as if she does not see Montserrat and a couple of steps further she goes back to her.

"Hi there," says Anna trying to face the music.

"Hi. How are you?" Montserrat struggles to sound completely calm.

"Fine, thank you," Anna utters with a sarcastic smile.

"Anna, look I'm sorry, this isn't going to work, OK?"

Anna, with a poker face, cannot believe what she hears.

Montserrat continues, "Did I ever explain to you why I broke up with that other woman? No? OK. I don't how it is for you in ... in theater with all your friends, all your artists ... but in science, in engineering it's different. When there's a school function it's husband and wife, man and woman, not woman and woman. Our society is not ready for that, OK?"

"Don't give me that crap!" Anna finally retorts.

"Can I ask you a question?" Montserrat asks Anna. Anna nods. Whatever she asks will not shock Anna more than she already is.

"Do you love me?" Montserrat asks.

"Yes, very much so," Anna replies completely unaffected.

"Then if you love me, why haven't you asked me to move in with you?" Montserrat asks.

Anna is speechless. The bells of the Temple Sagrada Familia put an end to the incoherent chat of both women on Gaudí Avenue.

Three hours later Montserrat has completed her move to Anna's place. The first thing she does is hang the fisherman's net she picked up at the Costa Brava on a white wall — recently painted. It takes them barely 30 minutes to have it right (or the way Montserrat thinks it is right). Montserrat's toothbrush is finally by Anna's.

Montserrat likes the spacious apartment. It has a quite sunny terrace. Generally, the access to it is through the dining room door, but more often than not Anna gains access to the terrace from the big window of a small room.

Anna sits by that windowsill, as Montserrat enters the terrace from the living room door. It is a good opportunity for Anna to check the time because as she sees Montserrat coming to the terrace, she suspects her working hours are over.

"What are you doing?" Montserrat asks leaning toward Anna.

"What?"

"What are you doing?"

"Fund raising."

"OK, let's raise some fun," replies Montserrat with a wry smile. Anna was right, fund raising time is over.

Chapter 10

Once you share your life with another person you know that there are things about this "significant other" that you like and then there are other things that you just happen to dislike. Anna loves all of Montserrat. All but these ridiculous red panties she has. Anna has never seen her wearing them, and hopes she never will. Anna just happens to have noticed them in her opened suitcase. They really make Anna furious. She hates them. She cannot understand why Montserrat has these hooky, flashy, red panties. She simply cannot. Anna is a woman of action and she believes in change. What would happen if she throws them through the window? So many pieces of clothing fall to her neighbors when she puts the laundry to sun dry! Who cares, one more piece? She decides to commit such felony and throw her lover's insidious panties through the window.

Anna is not the same since Montserrat has moved in with her and she knows it. Now Anna cooks. Sometimes Anna asks Montserrat to try her creations. "Montserrat?" Anna calls to her from the kitchen. Montserrat has just showered.

"Yeah?" replies Montserrat getting close to her. Anna offers her a spoonful of what she is cooking.

"Would you like to try this for me, please?"

"Not really."

"It's an invention."

"Yeah, it looks like it."

More often than not, they end up ordering pizza, but Anna tries.

In front of the mailbox, Anna feels utterly relieved. She is finally ready to mail all the grant applications. That means that she is done with the boring fund raising, now she just has to wait for the answers. As Anna thinks back, "Miguel Gasòliba, of course this name sounds familiar to me, wasn't he an ex-boyfriend of Marta's?"

Montserrat frantically searches the drawer of the

bedroom dresser. She looks for something with real interest. Anna tries to put the towels neatly into the cupboard. Since two people have to share all the utilities, she thinks she had better be tidier. Montserrat interrupts her thoughts. She sounds upset.

"Anna? Anna, have you seen my red panties?"

"What?"

"Have you seen my red panties?"

"Red?"

"Red, yes."

"No," Anna concedes.

All of a sudden, Montserrat finds photographs of Marta in the drawer. These are different size of black and white or color pictures of Marta L. Puig with Anna. One of them is dedicated to Anna.

"Who is she?" Montserrat asks Anna.

"Excuse me?"

"Who is she?"

Barely on time, they caught *Oedipus Queen*, the last show. They are at the Saint Andreu Theater. Montserrat attends a Catalan play for the first time. Anna ignores whether she will understand the language. In fact, Montserrat is more interested in studying Marta L. Puig closely.

Anna observes that Marta's voice has not changed a bit in all these years as she ends the first act.

"Oi Griselda, no m'ho facis això a mi dona, havia'm si us poseu d'acord d'una vegada, ara m'ho dius d'una manera, després m'ho dius d'una altre, havia'm, on sóc jo? On soc?"

[Griselda, don't do that to me ... make up your mind. Now you say one thing to me, then you say another ... tell me ... where? Where am I, where am I to you?]

Everybody in the audience raves and claps wildly. Some fans scream. Anna gets very upset and they decide to leave the theater. Montserrat is very satisfied by what she has seen.

"I loved her performance and I don't even understand Catalan," she says to a furious Anna.

"I'm gonna kill that bastard." Anna is really upset. Montserrat has to stop her.

"Wait! What's the matter?"

"What a disaster ... she's pathetic!" starts Anna.

"Oh, come on, you're just jealous ..."

"I'm not jealous. This set-designer-turned-director has killed her. I'm gonna kill that bastard."

"No, no, no, wait."

"I want a pizza now!"

On their way back home, Montserrat wants to know everything about the affair that Anna supposedly had with the Diva.

"So how is it that the Diva fell in love with you?"

"Well, she was drunk."

Montserrat needs to find out if that affair still haunts Anna. After all why does she still keep the photographs? "Did you suffer a lot when the two of you broke up?"

"No, not at all, it was very liberating." Anna's words ring true. Sometimes Montserrat cannot really tell when Anna acts and when she tells the truth. This time around she believes her.

At home, Anna, still dressed up, stands in the

kitchen looking at the playbill of *Oedipus Queen*. She shakes her head, still outraged by Marta's poor performance. She helps herself to a glass of juice when the bell rings. Montserrat goes to the door. Anna keeps shaking her head. Montserrat comes back to the kitchen. She is very happy and shows something to Anna.

"Honey look, the neighbors found my panties."

"That's wonderful," replies Anna trying to maintain her deadpan expression.

"Yeah!" agrees Montserrat. Montserrat goes to the bedroom completely enchanted with her new found panties.

Anna, in the kitchen, gets an idea. Montserrat needs a new key holder. A piece of visible red cloth to help her quickly notice where she left the keys. It would only take some knowledgeable use of scissors. Anna takes an acceptable pair of scissors, with a red handle. She goes about the red panties without Montserrat's consent.

They love going shopping together at the supermarket. It is not the shopping activity in itself as the "family" feeling they get when doing it together. Montserrat has also changed since the relationship started; at least she does things that she never did before. Sometimes she acts wild, like now. She dances with the shopping bags. She is a very different girl from the shy teacher Anna met at the Costa Brava.

Montserrat likes to make jokes now. Anna is interested to know how she will react when she sees her key holder with the magnificent red ribbon from her red flashy hooky panties attached to it. Anna thinks it is great. Everybody should have one. On the other hand, Anna is free from the horrendous bad taste red panties.

Anna kindly put the keys into the car's keyhole for Montserrat. A scream marks the exact moment when Montserrat makes eye contact with the new key holder.

"What have you done to my panties? I'm going to kill you!" It is her sentence that can be clearly heard throughout the parking lot. Obviously — although not understandably for Anna — Montserrat does not like the key holder. There is not much time to discuss it, however, because Anna has to start a tour in fifteen minutes.

Work is the same as usual. Tourists get crazy with their video cameras. "How's the videotaping going here, fine?" Anna asks. She wishes they could leave the cameras in the hotel and let themselves feel something of what they see when they stand in front of the gorgeous sites she takes them to. Anna has not had any news from the committees that award money for theater projects in Barcelona.

Whenever she allows the tourists to break for video time, her mind wanders "If I get one, just one grant, I'll be able to open the monologue in Barcelona. I miss the times when I used to rehearse, I miss that character."

Anna remembers the point of the monologue where her housewife first finds out she can identify with her lesbian neighbor. After a lot of thinking, Anna decided she would say that part sitting on a chair, while she polishes her red fingernails. On a chair, she could better work the pauses. Delivering the lines is important but silences are equally important for Anna, especially for her housewife character. Anna practiced what she called "affected silences." It is a particular kind of tense silence very common among Mediterranean housewives. Anna had no problems videotaping that part. The character would start polishing her fingernails and suddenly, the action was interrupted by a sound. As usual she would look straight into the camera with the Towers of the Sagrada Familia behind her.

"Ah! She's got a fax . . . she's got a fax machine. Very strange, every time a fax comes in, a music comes out, like a march or something . . . very quiet."

When she looks at the videotape at home, she notices the sound problems, but it is okay because when it gets really bad, she always drops a line to justify it.

"This is not her house."

and then she would resume her explanation about the first encounter she had with the neighbor.

". . . you know the other day, her fax machine was delivered, and she asked me if they could leave it with me. And I said, sure, of course, that's what neighbors are for, OK? And, when

I went over to her house, the next day to give her the fax machine, she invited me for a cup of tea ... Mmmmmm ... I hate tea. By ten we had already killed a bottle of whisky. Carlos was about to call the police. About. Barcelona football team was playing on TV. About to call. He has his priorities very clear.

"She told me the story of her life. What a woman, what she's been through, and she still keeps her high standards ... I felt very identified with her, with her spirit, with her push, with her ... ooomph."

Then the housewife would stand up and ramble around the rooftop up to the point where she would go back to the chair. By then, the housewife was ready for a crucial confession.

"You know, it's kind of funny. Every time she was looking straight to my eyes, I had to ... turn my eyes away. Then when I was able to look at her straight in the eyes, then ... my cramps started. Very ... something funny, very funny. Because that's very weird I mean ... I feel like I want something but I still don't know exactly what I want ... because I'm not a lesbian!"

At this point, the character makes the sign of the cross. The housewife was completely scandalized by only thinking that she might be a lesbian. That makes Anna wonder why the roads toward complete self-acceptance are so long. Just a couple of days ago, something similar happened to her and Montserrat. They were in the car and a tire had to be changed. They did it quite fast and to immortalize the moment, Montserrat set up her automatic camera just to finish the roll. On their way back home, Montserrat was silent. Then, all of a sudden, without being upset for anything specific she says, "I'm a lesbian . . . but that doesn't mean that I can't sleep with men every once in while."

Chapter 11

Montserrat's colleague at the University, Jordi, still goes after her. The interior decoration of this particular classroom has changed this semester. The students have taken the empty bottle out and now a small wooden bridge hangs from the ceiling. The class is over and Montserrat is still in the classroom when Jordi enters. He has a particular sense of humor. He takes his electronic organizer out of his pocket and looks at it. When Montserrat says "Hi" to him his answer is, "Correct, I'm here." Then he reads the screen of the organizer in an inexpressive tone. "The Dean's birthday party. Monday 28th."

Montserrat looks at him with a smile on her face. Before she can think of an excuse to decline, he shakes his head and shouts at her, "No way, it will be a Jewish religious holiday." Jordi switches the organizer off and he leaves the classroom.

Montserrat wants to tell Anna about Jordi but Anna has her mind on other concerns. Anna starts to get the answers from the committees that grant money for theater projects. She is being turned down by all of them. As soon as she gets a letter she glances at it very quickly . . . looking for the usual words "lament," "sorry," "unfortunately." When she detects those words, the reading stops and the letter goes straight to the garbage can. It is quite discouraging. For the first time in years, if not ever, Anna is depressed. She cannot see what action is left for her to take.

It is something new for her to see that all the doors she knocks at close in her face. Anna thinks about the guys she runs into when she goes to pick up all the application forms. Have they gotten any public money for their projects? Maybe somebody has. Most of them surely were rejected like she is. Montserrat does not realize the pain Anna is going through. All she sees is Anna closing in on herself. She does not communicate and she often cries without wanting to share it with Montserrat. Montserrat comes near her to inquire, "Anna, what is it?"

"Nothing, my life is going down the toilet, other than that, *'it's a wonderful life,'* " replies Anna.

If Anna cannot perform she does not feel very happy about anything else. Montserrat either does not understand, or she does understand and does not approve. In any case, Anna is positive that her downcast mood has helped Montserrat change her mind about the Dean's party.

The break in communication between both of them reaches a peak one day when Anna is pensive by the terrace and Montserrat watches her from the bedroom. Suddenly, Montserrat goes to the door of the bedroom and closes it slowly. Then she picks up the telephone in the bedroom. Trying not to be heard by Anna, Montserrat dials a number on the phone.

"Hello, Jordi? Hi, it's Montserrat. Jordi, you know, Monday is not a Jewish religious holiday. No, no I don't have to double check. OK. See you then. Bye." Montserrat hangs up and takes a deep breath. She is confused.

The day of the party arrives, and Anna takes it very calmly. Why should she take it any other way? Montserrat is out there with Jordi, right in the middle of Villa Olimpica, the new Barcelona, a part of the city built for the Olympic Games of 1992. It looks like the right place for engineers to gather. The buildings are all about structure and geometrical forms. There are triangles over some buildings or enormous metallic structures with the form of a fish to give a touch of who knows what to the ensemble of framework and glass. Anna hates that part of Barcelona.

Montserrat wears a dress. It took her and Jordi a while to find the restaurant, but finally they arrive at the party. The Dean came with the secretary of the school and his daughter. Montserrat's colleague, Carme Coll, also came to the party with her daughter.

Anna is at her apartment. She remembers how many times Montserrat has asked her opinion whether she should go to the Dean's party with Jordi or not.

"Jordi?" Anna had to refresh her memory. "Jordi? Oh, Jordi! That Jordi!"

Anna does some Tai-Chi, that is, closely follows a Tai-Chi manual and tries to forget about Montserrat and Jordi. "I love Tai-Chi," she says to herself. "Every time I feel like . . . killing somebody . . . I do some Tai-Chi."

In the meantime at the party, all the Dean's guests must listen to his non-stop monologues. Carme Coll feels particularly out of place. Montserrat has a problem with the smoke and requests to get out of there for a moment. Jordi and she leave the restaurant and go out by the boats. They sit and Jordi starts a conversation. Montserrat is having a good time.

Anna remains at home by herself. She is finished with the Ta- Chi and now she eats a pizza. She will finish it before Montserrat gets back. Her mind works as fast as her jaw. "If at least I could make a couple funny lines out of it. OK. Happiness is like a well balanced diet, you get to eat pasta some days, with no sauce. Now, if you're in love with a person who is bisexual, then happiness becomes indigestion."

Jordi and Montserrat watch the boats in the marina. A part of the Villa reminds Montserrat of New York's Fulton Fish Market. All of a sudden, she notices a fisherman's blue net on the ground. It looks like an anachronism because no fisherman's boat is near them. The area is a very urban area, nothing in common with the wilderness of the Costa Brava. Montserrat remembers Anna's words, "Nothing, my life is going down the toilet, other than that..." Jordi realizes how far away her mind must be and he suggests they leave.

Anna sits on the bed and plays with a small replica of the earth. Montserrat comes into the apartment. Her high heels can be heard from the bedroom. She is in a very bad mood. "What a waste of time. You should have talked me out of going."

At this point, Anna improvises a quick monologue. "No way, you haven't reached bottom yet. You still think you'd be better off with a man. You wanna try it again with a guy? Go ahead be my guest."

Anna is sitting on the bed and Montserrat starts undressing. Anna goes on. "Now, when you realize that he has blasted your dreams, that he has nullified you as a human being that you've achieved security but yeah, ha, ha, security, security, my eyes, security through sacrificing your career, then you'll reach bottom, and then you'll say, 'I wish I'd never had gone to that party.'"

Finally Montserrat throws her top at Anna.

"Damn," replies Anna.

"Bravo," Montserrat concedes.

Chapter 12

Everything is back to normal. Anna loves Montserrat more than anything else, and Montserrat loves Anna. Anna goes to the Faculty of Engineering to pick Montserrat up when she finishes work and they go together back home. Every time they can, they take the alleys of Hospital of Saint Paul, one of Anna's favorite spots in Barcelona.

"You know, sometimes I have doubts about us, but basically I think I love you very much," Anna tells Montserrat.

"Well, I think we're made for each other, even though ..."

"You think so?"

"Even though ... you're terrible in bed, you're an egocentric bitch, you never let me know what's going on, you don't like to have sex that much, let's see, what else?"

"No but when I wanna have sex, I'm very good, you say that and you say other kinds of things."

"Yes, when you wanna have sex you're very good, you're right, you're right, what was I thinking? I mean we're perfect for each other!"

"Yeah I think so. I think you like sex a little bit too much, that's the only problem."

What Anna has long realized now is that you first fall in love with a person, and then you get to know her. The person can be very different from what you first figured. Fortunately they are getting used to each other.

The Temple of the Sagrada Familia has yet to be finished. The tourists look at it with amazement as Anna addresses the rest of the group on Gaudí Avenue. She tries to do her job the best she can. She even gives some insights to the tourists, especially when they ask about the "siesta," that nap that people in Spain used to take.

"Well this is a little bit of a cliche, I would say that this is not, you know, 'siesta country.' I mean Catalonia. Because, you see people here are very busy, all the time, they do twenty things at the same time, they won't relax until they finish them all, and they never finish them all, so they are always tense."

This morning, like any other morning, during the break Anna tries once more to reach, by phone, Miguel Gasòliba. With his business card in her hand, she dials the number. She already knows it by heart. It is all in vain. Miguel Gasòliba, Marta's ex-lover, does not take her calls. He is the last chance to open the monologue in Barcelona. He is the chairperson of the only selection committee that has not rejected her project yet.

Anna no longer rehearses the piece. She considers that the monologue has some very good moments. The scene where the housewife explains her latest nightmare to the audience came out quite nice on the videotape that Anna sent to San Francisco. The housewife comes with an empty bucket, talking straight to the camera.

"I had a nightmare last night. I was on top of the Eiffel Tower, France, and my neighbor — the lesbian — was on top of the Sagrada Familia in Barcelona. Awful. No, there was no tea.

"I was on top of the Eiffel Tower asking the world why women — even if we're more efficient, smarter, and more intelligent than men — why — because I see it at the subway station. Why do we get a lower status and a lower salary. Why?

"And my neighbor — the lesbian — she answered me from the top of the Sagrada Familia in Barcelona. She said it was all because of the outrageous satisfaction that you're supposed to get through the orgasm from penetration. I didn't understand a thing and I said . . . wait a minute, I know everything about penetration. I know that the orgasm through penetration is statistically insignificant. Damn!"

And she would leave the frame.

Anna likes to recreate these moments but she has to work. Back to reality, surrounded by international tourists, she allows herself to improvise on almost any question she is asked. For example, on the differentiated personality of Catalonia from the rest of Spain her answer is "OK, Catalonia is a small and peculiar country, OK. That's a very personal opinion but I always say that whatever reason made the United States to be the powerful country it is today, it's too simple a reason to be understood by the sophistication of a Catalan mind."

The Dean at the School of Engineering is after something. He has an envelope in his hands. He looks for Carme Coll's mail box. When he finds it, he drops the letter.

Montserrat is out of the faculty to have lunch. When she comes back she runs into Carme Coll at the main entrance. At first, Montserrat does not pay attention to her. Then she recognizes Carme Coll behind her sunglasses. Carme carries a box with personal belongings. She has been fired.

Chapter 13

One of the nicest things about Barcelona is the permanent kind of weather. Compared to New York, Barcelona's weather is a blessing; it is like a year-long spring. Montserrat gives herself a pedicure on the sunny terrace of the apartment. Anna is inside and is not in a good mood. She is not communicative since so many rejections weigh on her. Montserrat, on the contrary, is talkative today as she sits at the windowsill.

"A friend of mine at the faculty has been fired and she won't be the only one. Are you listening to me?" Montserrat insists.

"Excuse me?"

"Did you call Miguel?"

"Yes."

"And?"

"He's not taking my calls."

"Well look, then why don't you just forget it? I know you didn't ask me but I think you've done everything you can to get the money and I just think you ought to forget it. You're becoming obsessed with this opening in Barcelona. There's more to life than just theater . . . you look at me. I'm not goal-oriented the way you are. I only live to be able to work, no, you live to be able to work, I only work to be able to live."

"Well then go to California."

"Oh great. Your problem is that you're just like a man, the only difference is that you don't have a penis between your legs," Montserrat throws at Anna.

"Excuse me? I act like a man, just because I pursue my dreams? You know what you've just said? That's what a man would have said. You think like a man, that's what you do."

"Well you're being rough on me."

Anna does not like the tone of the conversation. From now on, she clowns around. Now she is about to jump through their bedroom window. "How cruel of you saying that to me, I'm going to kill myself now," Anna screams at Montserrat.

"Don't start, will you? Don't start, stop it."

"I'm going to kill myself now."

"Oh, go kill yourself, you're nuts anyway."

"Yeah, schizophrenic, that's what you become when you go out with a bisexual."

"Oh, so now it's my fault that you're crazy? Anna, let me tell you something . . . seriously, seriously though. You're one of the few people I've known that really needs psychoanalysis."

"What?"

Anna comes back to Montserrat on her knees to get closer to her. "See what I mean?" Montserrat says. Anna is still impressed by what Montserrat said about psychoanalysis.

"Oh!" Anna gets distracted by the small pieces of cotton put between each toe of Montserrat's foot. Then she goes back to the impact made on her by the line about psychoanalysis. "I like that. That's . . . witty. Is that yours?"

"All mine."

"I loved it."

"Good."

"Oh, it's very good."

"Yeah, yeah, yeah."

"May I use it sometime? It certainly would make a very funny line for a smart character."

"Yes, please."

"Marta and I used to talk like that all the time . . ."

Just when she has said it, she regrets having made the comment. Montserrat does not ignore the remark.

"Yeah, well maybe Marta would make Miguel take your phone calls."

"No."

"Why not?"

"What? No."

"Why not? Look at you, look at you. You're still obsessed with that relationship, you think I'm stupid. I'm not stupid, you're still obsessed about that relationship."

Obviously, Anna has to think of something to solve this and think fast. "Lunch for three?"

"Lunch for three," Montserrat concedes.

"Would you like to have lunch for three?" Anna repeats like a small boy while leaning toward a very upset Montserrat.

Fixing the lunch date with the Diva was easier than Anna thought it would be. The three of them, Montserrat, the Diva, and Anna, are at The Villa Olimpica. Marta is dressed all in white. She always dresses extravagantly. For the first time, Marta and Montserrat meet. The Diva is as sarcastic as Anna, if not more. Anna is intrigued — and fearful — to see what Marta's attitude will be toward Montserrat. Anna knows she can be a bitch. Maybe it is because of this fear that Anna acts like a spoiled brat while walking along the sunny avenues of this seaside Barcelona area.

"I want a pizza please . . ." Anna begs.

"It doesn't make any difference to me," points out Montserrat.

"Don't be so American, let's go to a seafood restaurant," Marta says.

Anna disagrees, "There's a twenty-minute wait."

Marta insists, "We can wait, there's plenty of time."

"But I like pizza, Marta," Anna says, behaving like a five-year-old.

They walk along the avenue until a decision is made. To kill time, Marta makes conversation. "And what were you doing in New York, killing roaches or counting roaches?" It is so obvious that she could not care less. Anna notices it.

Montserrat answers, "She was getting her M.F.A. in Drama at Columbia."

"At Columbia! Everybody goes to Columbia these days," Marta dismisses.

"Well, that's where she toured her show. She toured some universities and . . ." Montserrat becomes Anna's lawyer.

"I want a pizza," Anna repeats.

Montserrat wants to go to business. "And now she's writing a play . . . right, Anna?"

"A monologue," Anna points out.

"A monologue. Excuse me."

"A monologue . . . everybody does monologues," Marta concludes.

"And she's trying to open in Barcelona, right, Anna?"

Montserrat tries to get Anna to plead with Marta to help her. It seems that Montserrat and Marta both get along quite well. "Oh listen, I loved your performance in this play," Montserrat says.

"Oh, I hated it . . . I hated it . . . I think the set-designer-turned-director has killed you, if I can be honest," Anna says.

Montserrat wants to make peace. She places

herself between Marta and Anna. "OK. OK. Listen, you two, look. You two are friends, right? If you two are friends, can't you help each other out? You know Miguel, right?"

"I know Miguel," says Marta.

"Could you make him take her calls?" Montserrat acts like the quintessential peacemaker and Anna sees that.

"OK, I'll fix it, don't worry," Marta concedes.

"Well thank you," Anna concludes with a tone half between true appreciation and pure sarcasm.

"Let's go eat," suggests Montserrat.

"Pizza!" demands Anna.

The area is famous for the seafood restaurants but they manage to find a pizzeria. Anna's craving for a pizza shows she is more tense than she would actually like to be.

After lunch the fresh air does Montserrat and Anna good. Marta has to rush to rehearsals for her next play and runs out. Anna is pensive. She remembers how strongly Montserrat has defended her in front of Marta. Anna feels very touched by it. She suddenly stops and looks at Montserrat. Montserrat comes closer to Anna.

"Nobody has ever loved me as much as you do," Anna concedes with an almost broken voice. Montserrat smiles, with that irresistible smile of hers. All of a sudden, in the midst of this romantic mood, it occurs to Anna that she has been trying to get public money from institutions but that she has never tried the most direct way.

"Theater producers, I still haven't tried them. Damn!"

Montserrat takes it as well as she can. She

already knows Anna and she is hardly ever surprised by any of her unexpected reactions. Anna's lyrical *momento* turned into a renewed push in her fund raising efforts.

Back at her job, Anna is at the bus terminal. She decides to start right away the strategy to get funding for her monologue. As soon as she has a break she goes to a pay phone. She starts dialing the numbers of independent producers.

Anna has a problem. It is a French problem. There is a terribly antsy French tourist who simply cannot stay still for a second. The tourists who have the obsession of using every possible minute of their time are the worst. They very often get lost and then the rest of the troupe has to change the schedule because of them. Anna, while on the phone, has to address herself in an energetic way to the French tourist.

"Madame, arrêtez là, oui" [Madam, stop here].

Even though Anna tries to use her best French accent, the tone shows she is really pissed off by the tourist. *"La mare que la va,"* says Anna to herself, referring to the tourist's mother in Catalan language. Finally somebody gets on the telephone. She is about to talk to a theater producer.

"Ah, hola," Anna says to the producer.

Again the French woman is about to split. *"Madame, ça va chauffeur, oui. Arretêz la s'il vous plait on va partir dans cinc minutes, d'acord? Merci, eh?"* [Madame, enough is enough. Stop right there please, we leave in 5 minutes, OK? Thank you?]

"Eh?" Again when she attends the phone call she does not use the most professional tone. That is why she decides to take some time to focus on what she is doing for her career. Anna has to address the person who is on the line, a person who can give her financing for the monologue. Unfortunately, Anna does not have, at this point, the calm necessary when dealing with these people.

"Hola, escolti vostes llegeixen coses? Ah si si . . . gracias" [Do you read things?] The answer she is given is so assertive and complex that the person monopolizes the entire conversation. Anna can only answer, "yes . . . yes . . . yes . . . yes . . . thank you." Time is running out, she has to make more phone calls. She drops the phone, then the telephone will not take her coins. The French lady really drives Anna out of her mind. She is now really upset with the tourist. *"Madam, arretêz là* [Madame, stop here]!"

When she finally gets to talk to all of the producers, Anna gets an answer that she does not like at all. She is really down and out. The producers say that a monologue from a housewife's point of view is of no interest whatsoever. That kind of rejection hurts. The working day is over and she walks, downcast by, the gigantic Barcelona Football Club Stadium.

At the faculty of Engineering things do not look any brighter. The Dean is tense. Every time he has to fire somebody, he gets tense. Deep down, he is a sentimental guy. He likes his personnel, especially Montserrat. The Dean looks for her. He has a letter in his hands and the letter is for her. He does not want to simply put the letter in Montserrat's box. He feels he owes her an explanation. He wants to tell her how many budget cuts he has had this year and the number of projects that will have to be postponed because of them. The most painful part is that he has yet to fire more instructors. The Dean enters the Mechanics Laboratory where he usually finds Montserrat, but she is not there. He will try the main classroom. Just when he is about to enter the classroom with the letter addressed to Montserrat, she sees him. Definitely, she does not want to run into him. Montserrat always runs and hides from the Dean.

Anna enters the faculty. She wears her tennis shoes and has her red umbrella with her. Women do not wear tennis shoes with skirts in Barcelona, but Anna saw New York women doing it and adopted the habit. People stare at her constantly because of that. When she finally finds Montserrat in an empty classroom, she is about to tell her about her fiasco when Jordi enters the room. Jordi is very tense. He says how sorry he feels for her. At this point, both Montserrat and Anna are shocked. Jordi explains that everybody got very surprised when the Dean told them that Montserrat was the next person to be fired.

Anna helps Montserrat pack away all her personal belongings and they exit the faculty of Engineering with boxes and blueprints.

"What were you saying about feeling rejected?" inquires Montserrat in a sardonic tone.

Now they are both in very similar stages. Anna tries to find all the positive angles to the present situation. She is quite good at it if she pushes herself to do so. They talk in the dining room under the fisherman's net they hung up on the wall.

"Montserrat, if you hate teaching, don't look for a teaching job. Why don't you look for a job in research?"

Montserrat fears change, and more than change, inactivity. Anna senses that and sets up intense brainstorm sessions. She is determined to help Montserrat put her life back on track again. They spend hours figuring out what to do. For Montserrat, explaining the basics of her research to Anna helps her clarify her mind.

"Mechanics is what I taught in both Tel Aviv and Barcelona but the main line of my research was seismic response of structural materials. In fact, now that I think about it I started out focused on 'S.A.'"

Anna does not have a clue what Montserrat is saying but she patiently listens to her anyway. Montserrat realizes that Anna does not understand terms like "S.A." and she clarifies it for her.

"I'm sorry, Seismic Analysis — but shortly after, I went for structural design for earthquake resistance. Oh." Montserrat shows her a sample, "This was pre-cast concrete cladding detail. I determined a method of S.A. on pre-cast concrete bridges three years ago."

Anna gets the picture. Montserrat got sidetracked by teaching while her motivation was S.A. research. It is crystal clear for Anna that Montserrat has to pursue, at any price, a career in research. She understands Montserrat very well, for what would Anna do without theater?

Walking up and down St. Paul Hospital always fills up Anna's soul with hope and joy; the beauty of the pavilions is such. She expects the hospital to have the same effect on Montserrat, but Montserrat is on the verge of serious depression. Sitting on a bench, Montserrat inquires with not much hope, "OK, who does research on seismic analysis?"

"All you need is the names, right ... of the companies who do research?"

"Right, how do we get the ..."

"All you need is information ..."

"Information is a privilege in this country, that's what you've always said, isn't it?"

"Yeah, but privilege number one is to be a Catalan, and I'm a Catalan." Anna knows at this point what precise steps to take. She just needed a statement from Montserrat, a sign that proved that Montserrat had finally made up her mind about what she wanted to do in life. Anna ignores that the whole thing was even easier than that because Montserrat knew all along that she wanted to do research. All she needed was the courage to take action. Her being fired from the school of engineering has certainly helped her.

Anna knows a guy who works at one of the most prestigious private business schools in Barcelona. The library of the school does first class network research, not only about universities, but about public and private business and companies from all over the world. The business school should be their next step.

Once at the library, Anna lets Montserrat work with the man. He is an attractive young man of about twenty-five, wearing a business suit and a tie. The man sits at the computer and Montserrat, wearing her best clothes, stands beside him. Both of them look at the screen. "Please try to be really generic for me," the man says to Montserrat.

"OK. Seismic response," indicates Montserrat and the man types the two words. Montserrat's face shows terror when she reads the number of entries produced with the two words. "Three hundred?"

"That's my first entry," he calms her.

"Sorry."

In the meantime, Anna is on the phone ordering Champagne

"I'd like to order Champagne. Cases, not bottles, cases." It is a Catalan thing to pay back favors with something substantial.

Montserrat gives the man a more precise term so that the number of the potential companies who do research in seismic analysis decreases. "Your second one could be concrete structures."

"Fifty. Would you like me to be more selective? Pre-cast? Pre-stressed?"

"Pre-cast!" Montserrat says with a strong determination typical of somebody really versed in the field.

"Specific structures if any?"

"Bridges."

"OK. Twenty."

They had done a great job. From 300 possible companies more or less related to seismic analysis they ended up with 20 companies with a research department devoted exclusively to Montserrat's area of expertise.

Back at home they discuss every possible angle. They confer in bed.

"OK, twenty companies. Now what?" asks Montserrat.

"OK, how many companies do you have?"

"Twenty. Twenty companies."

"Yeah? Where are they located?"

"In the U.S. and in New Zealand."

"Where?"

"U.S. and New Zealand."

"Let's screen the companies."

"OK. How do we screen them?"

Chapter 14

Some people reach a point in their lives where the most dull and uninteresting activities done in the past become excruciatingly useful. That is the case for Anna. At present, she is dressed in her tour guide uniform with a sportive Montserrat going through Anna's photo album from her New York years. They are on a break from Anna's work and they both enjoy, once more, a sunny day of gorgeous Mediterranean weather. Anna makes comments as she shows the photos to Montserrat.

"That's in my office at the Hispanic advertising

agency in New York. I look much better now. I was miserable. There's nothing worse in life than working in an advertising agency. Oh, that's Daniel Stein, my favorite account executive. He used to handle the roach killer account."

At last her years in New York working in advertising are worth something useful. Screening the companies means, as Anna puts it, "to find out which ones you can trust and which ones you can't." Generally, that is a job that people pay to have done, except for Anna. Thanks to Daniel Stein, they would have this information for free. "Daniel Stein works on Wall Street now. He'll screen those companies for us. He's a darling."

They decide to fax Daniel the list of the twenty companies right away. Maybe the whole thing will work out.

Back on the job, Anna is in the middle of Gaudí Avenue trying to concentrate as she addresses the tourists, but she cannot. "OK guys, I have a problem. Well I have more than one, but anyway..." She cannot concentrate because she remembers what is happening in her life. If she could tell the tourists what her *real* problems are...

"My problem number one is that the woman I'm in love with is looking for a job in New Zealand, or in the U.S." Just two hours ago, Anna was at the terrace hanging an Italian camafeo on the wall when Montserrat came in really excited. She had a fax in her hands. "It's the fax from Daniel! Twelve companies. Twelve companies and they're all in the U.S. He says there's only twelve companies trustworthy."

"That's great."

"Damn!" says Montserrat imitating Anna's accent.

She would tell the tourists her other concerns in her relationship, "Problem number two. We are happy, but we also have our differences." Last Saturday, they were both cleaning the terrace. Anna felt weird, and she knew why. They had been together for some time now and Anna found that these "cleaning episodes" were not very usual. Maybe they should do it more often, the cleaning. Anna started to suspect that she was doing more house cleaning than Montserrat was. Anna had to make a comment to Montserrat about this.

"I find it very funny that you say sometimes that I behave like a man, and then I'm the one who gets to do the house cleaning, *always*."

"No comment."

Deep down, Anna never accepted what she had to hear from Montserrat about her "behaving like a man." Anna hated roles.

These two were only part of Anna's problems in life. There were even more problems to keep to herself. "My problem number three . . . my chances of opening in Barcelona look ugly. Miguel Gasòliba is not taking my calls. And the only one who can make him take my calls is the ex-love of my life, Marta L. Puig."

Anna remembers the encounter of the two with the Diva. As they rambled while deciding what to eat, Montserrat did all she could to get the Diva's involvement in Anna's fund raising efforts.

"She sent the proposal to some guy, right Anna?" said Montserrat.

"Yeah, Miguel Gasòliba."

"Oh Miguel, Miguel, he always chickens out..." said Marta.

Anna says to Montserrat, "He's an ex-boyfriend of hers..."

"Well, he's a friend of mine, so what happened with Miguel?" asked Marta.

The number of the Diva's lovers was almost as huge as the Barcelona phone book. Anna always suspected that the Diva also went out with men every now and then for a statistical reason, just to justify her bisexuality.

Definitely, Anna is not in a positive mood today. Instead of focusing on the good things that are happening to her and Montserrat, she has decided to make an inventory of her problems.

"Problem number four. My chances of going to the U.S. with my monologue are very slim. I have a copy at home of the videotape I sent to Another Stage in San Francisco. The sound is awful. There's too much background noise from the church and I blow every punch line."

She is right on that one. Every time she looks at the tape she gets mad. The sound is not the best ever, but yet her performance comes through as fresh, and personal. Anna feels sad because her favorite part of *Love Thy Neighbor* did not come out as good as she wanted it to. It is the part where the housewife explains the second conversation she has had with the lesbian neighbor of hers. The housewife considers the neighbor a friend, and through their conversations, the housewife comes out as a bright woman.

"We had another chat. She was going on and on about the male oriented world of psycho-analysis, semantics, pragmatics, syntactics, and all that crap.

"And I was impressing her with my comments on it all. Yeah, because sometimes she gets some kind of boring you know ... All the time she was telling me about the importance of having a dick ... except that no ... she calls it something else, the pen ... no ... the phallus! The phallus!

" 'Never mind all these big words, it's simple. Have you ever seen a guy trying to find a parking slot in midtown? Sweaty face, red eyes, panting, getting desperate ... he drives around in circles ... so the thing is once you have it' where to park it?" And she was very impressed."

Anna thinks that she mispronounced the sentence. "I should have said, 'Where do you park it?'" and this has been bothering her for weeks now.

The problem of problems, the one that stands at the very highest point is ... Montserrat's sexual ambiguity. Yesterday was a hot day and they took a break before parking the car. Montserrat spotted her automatic camera and in order to finish the roll, she decided to take a picture of them. The truth is that they were not looking very feminine. Montserrat looks at Anna straight in the eyes and started that old familiar song with resignation, "I'm a lesbian ... but . . . never mind."

In fact, it was a turning point. For the first time, Anna noticed that the issue about to be or not to be (a lesbian) lost Montserrat's interest. Maybe Montserrat was starting to accept herself or her sexual orientation. Anna knew very well that she herself had to go through the same thing and that it took quite a long time for her to accept it.

Anna talks in front of the group of tourists telling them everything about Gaudí. In her mind she goes back to Montserrat. "Let's go back to problem number one. Montserrat is working on her presentation."

Anna is right. Montserrat works really hard on putting together all her blueprints, published articles, research data, graphic materials, everything she needs for a stunning presentation. Anna thinks about her. "I know she's going to get a job in the U.S. She's all brains. Brains and libido." Fortunately the tour is about to end. "So, yes, ladies and gentlemen I have problems. I have big problems, I have small problems, I have identity problems . . . I have problems up to my . . . eyes." Anna fears that one day she may turn her bad temper against the tourists. Miraculously that has not happened yet.

Chapter 15

Montserrat goes to Saint Paul Hospital to see if by any chance she can catch Anna with the tourists. Montserrat is eager to show Anna the presentation she has put together for each one of the twelve U.S. companies that have been screened. She does find Anna by the Gynecology Pavilion. Anna checks her tourists' list.

"What's up?"

"Look what I have. This is my presentation. What do you think?" Montserrat shows Anna a folder with documents and Anna glances at it with intense attention.

"And the references?"

"Pretty good eh?"

"Yeah . . ."

"What do you think?"

"Well, now you have to write the most powerful cover letter ever."

They come back home. The next hours and days are devoted to the writing and rewriting of what can open Montserrat's doors to make her dream come true. Anna sweeps the terrace when Montserrat comes to her with her latest draft of the cover letter. Montserrat reads it to Anna who does not say a word until Montserrat finishes.

" 'Looking forward to hearing from you, Sincerely Yours, Montserrat Ehrzman-Rosas.' What do you think?"

"Ah . . . very good . . . there's only one thing," Anna plays with the broom. "Since English is your first language, couldn't you do it a little bit more business- like, just a little bit more concise, more profound, more professional, like down to the point, like clearer, you state clearly what you want . . . without so much redundance and . . . but basically it's a magnificent effort. Well, do it again!"

Montserrat is exhausted. She writes it over and over. Anna is very picky, but Montserrat knows that she is right. If Montserrat has to work for American people, they have to see from moment one that she expresses herself like one of them. Had she been looking for a job in Spain, the strategy would have been completely different.

At last, Montserrat gets to put into the mail the twelve presentations. Secretly, Anna fears the worst, that they will have to part ways. "The countdown has just started. Montserrat's presentations will reach the twelve U.S. companies in seven days."

Anna reads one of her favorite acting manuals. As far as she is concerned there is nothing better than Stanislavsky's manuals. Montserrat enters the room and joins Anna in bed where, as usual, a new top-level conference takes place.

Montserrat asks, "Now what do we do?"

Anna says, "Well, say a little prayer, and take some vacation . . . to Girona for instance."

Anna cannot leave her job and Montserrat cannot stay without doing anything so the vacation concept becomes very useful. Anna makes sure that Montserrat knows how to get to Girona, and that Montserrat visits all the streets that should be seen.

Chapter 16

Montserrat is finally in Girona. She visits the venerable Jewish gravestones. Girona has a very important collection of Hebrew documents from the Middle Ages. In this city, various Jewish philosophers and cabalists, like Nahmanides, were born. Some of the streets resemble the streets of Jerusalem. They are called *El Call* [Jewish ghetto]. The old houses are built over the Jewish old houses, which is why some big rocks on the walls have mezuzahs carved on them even though they are not at the entry of the house nor by any door.

As Montserrat sees the old medieval patios and the mezuzahs she cannot help remembering all the people who have since long talked to her about Girona. The first one was Anna the same day they met at the Costa Brava. "If you're Jewish, you should visit the Medieval Jewish Ghetto in Girona. Girona? 'G' 'I' 'R' 'O' 'N' 'A,' Girona." Anna hurriedly spelled the name of the city for her. Anna loved Girona. She always said that people speak Catalan with an exquisite and authentic accent in Girona.

As she walks up Cundaro Street, Montserrat notices an elevated corridor crossing the street. She had read that through those corridors Jewish people escaped from persecutors, especially at Easter. Jordi, of course, had also suggested that Montserrat go to Girona. Montserrat remembers it. "You're Jewish? Montserrat, I'm going to take you to Girona. When are we going?"

Even the Diva mentioned Girona to her. In fact, the Diva had always been very nice toward her. Montserrat wishes that Marta and Anna would get along.

"Are you shefardi?" Marta asked Montserrat.

"Yes."

"You should visit Girona, the Jewish ghetto."

"Everybody tells her so," said Anna.

"Anna . . ."

Montserrat notices some gorgeous gardens where most probably one of the synagogues once stood. She recalls how easily she told the story of her life to Anna when they met, "no . . . my grandparents fled the Nazis and they stayed at the Monastery in Montserrat and they just thought it was a great name and they gave it to me." Montserrat is not somebody very given to telling her life story. Anna kept silent and listened to her. She has never seen Anna so silent since then.

"I was born in Tel Aviv and then at seven my parents moved to Boston, I was raised in Boston but I lived in New York for a while as well."

"Where in New York?"

Only when mentioning New York, Anna seemed to come back to life.

Montserrat finds Girona extremely beautiful but she takes the first opportunity to give Anna a ring. She finds a telephone at the Centre Bonastruc ça Porta, the Jewish Museum in Girona. She dials the number. Fortunately Anna is back home. She picks up the receiver at once.

"*Digueu?*"

"Hi. It's beautiful."

"You love it?"

"Yes. The Tramuntana wind, though, is not the same without you, honey." Montserrat sounds really nice but not even the most sensual of voices can make Anna forget the basics.

"Hmmmm. Are you wearing a scarf?"

"Oh, Anna, please!"

The next day, Montserrat lies in bed while Anna, about to go to work, gives her a good bowl of chicken soup. "Come on, Montserrat."

The Temple of the Sagrada Familia is constantly crowded by groups of tourists. Gaudí worked on it until 1926 when a trolley ran over him and he died. Anna is about to give the generic speech about Gaudí and Barcelona but she cannot get out of her mind the thought of being stuck with her theatrical project. The punch line of her monologue keeps popping into her mind.

" 'So the thing is, once you have it, where to park it?' And she was very impressed."

Anna studies different possibilities while touring Barcelona. For her, it is a given that Montserrat will eventually find herself a job in the U.S. "If I open in Barcelona, I'll make some money and then, I'll join Montserrat in the U.S!"

After all, she figures, the monologue *Love Thy Neighbor* should please the selection committee of the very prestigious Another Stage. The monologue is very clear in certain issues. The heterosexual housewife would eventually make love to the (lesbian) neighbor. That part came out very well on the tape sent to Another Stage.

The housewife was presented for the first time without a jacket, her hair was uncombed. She definitely looked "human," and more vulnerable as opposed to the charicaturesque archetype she embodied before. That vulnerability made her look far more attractive than before. As usual, the housewife spoke straight to the camera, as if the camera was the audience. She was a woman in distress.

"Don't ask me what happened . . . all I know is that I was depressed because of the holes of my parking slot theory, she was depressed too because the Mayor of Barcelona was not calling her to start working...we started both crying, then...then...I, I hugged her and two hours later, we were taking a shower.

"I never knew sex could be tender...You know with Carlos is fine, I mean I love it. But it's kind of a rudimentary satisfaction, you know...with her, it was great!"

Anna misses the rehearsals and the more she missed them, the more she catches herself replaying the monologue in her mind. She realizes, on the other hand, that the Diva is not making the phone call for her so that Miguel Gasòliba will take her calls. "Marta is not helping me with Miguel. Marta," Anna concludes.

Anna gets more and more angry. She notices, suddenly, that in the monologue the neighbor at the end has to leave Barcelona. Is it just a coincidence or a sign?

A sick Montserrat starts to feel pretty bored at home. She has only caught a cold, but Anna told her that a cold badly cured can lead to a pneumonia. Dozing around the place, Montserrat finally decides to play some videos and lies on the sofa. To her surprise, she discovers Anna's tape of Love Thy Neighbor and is overwhelmed.

"She's going back to Madrid, to reopen her office. 'You have a home there,' she told me. I might go...my suspicions about Carlos were right, he was seeing another woman. Yesterday he said, 'I had an affair with another woman but it is over now,' and I said, 'Oh yeah? Well, so did I.' "

Montserrat smiles. It was by reading this monologue that she started to feel interest for Anna. Now she sees it on a tape and Anna is stuck with it without getting funds to open in Barcelona. Montserrat's smile vanishes. She decides she must do something about it.

On the coffee table she sees Miguel Gasòliba's business card. She must act quickly. She does not care about the cold. She leaves the apartment and goes straight to the SAT theater. She has no clue about when the Diva has to come in. She might not even show up today. At any rate, she just has to ask.

Montserrat thinks about all that is going on when she hears a specific sound of high heels on the pavement. She turns around. The Diva is about to cross the street. She has a script and a bottle of water in her hands. Montserrat tries to stay calm. The Diva has always been very kind to her. It will work out.

"Marta!" Montserrat finally yells.

The Diva turns and when she recognizes Montserrat, she puts on her widest smile. Montserrat holds Miguel Gasòliba's card very strongly for when the moment comes that she will hand it over to the Diva.

Feeling like a character in a silent movie comedy, Montserrat rushes back to bed just when Anna rings the bell. Montserrat fears being discovered.

"What's up? How are you feeling?"

"OK . . ."

Anna puts her hand in Montserrat's forehead "You're sweaty! I'm gonna take your temperature, OK?" Anna does not pursue her action because the telephone rings. *"Sí?"*

Miguel Gasòliba is on the line.

In the area of Barcelona called Montjuich, one of Anna's favorites, Miguel Gasòliba has one of his offices. He is on so many selection committees that he has offices all over the city. The building is Art Nouveau, what in Barcelona is called Modernista and again, Anna adores the style for its decadence and mannerism or even better for its excess. Everything about Modernism is excessive, even the beauty. Anna, being the obsessive type, thinks Modernism was made just for her. She likes rounded forms over straight lines, delicate ornamentations over utilitarian designs. She thinks about all that in a semi-conscious manner while waiting for Miguel Gasòliba to invite her into his office.

She is tense. She knows this is the last chance she has to open the monologue in Barcelona. On the other hand, she tells herself to relax because everything that had to be done is already done. There is absolutely nothing else that she can do, so why be tense? So what if her only way out was to perform in the U.S? Isn't she crazy about the U.S? She always has been, after all. The only problem would be that since she met Montserrat she is starting to feel so much at home at the Costa Brava.

Right before she goes onto thinking about the Tramuntana wind, the door of Miguel Gasòliba's office opens. He appears, affable, walking toward her, with an amiable smile, and at once he excuses himself for not being able to answer her phone calls. Usually sudden trips to Madrid are the most common excuse to justify the unjustifiable in Barcelona, and Miguel Gasòliba quickly goes for that one.

Anna, walking with him toward the office, has no alternative but to accept his excuses and even believe them out of necessity. Not to believe him would mean to accept that she is of no interest at all for him and therefore her project has no chance to open in Barcelona.

Montserrat is back in bed, but not for long. Her interesting car key holder is on the small bedroom table, near the Kleenex. Montserrat cannot help thinking what Miguel Gasòliba would tell Anna about the monologue. After so much declining to take her phone calls he cannot change his mind toward her material overnight and help her out. Montserrat thinks the worst. Finally, she picks up the keys of her car and leaves the bed.

Anna is on her way out of the building. Miguel Gasòliba did not like the play — he meant monologue. Under these circumstances in certain countries, if a person like him does not like the monologue, there will be no monologue. That is to say — no funding.

Why he did not like it is something Anna did not have the guts to ask. She was pretty sure of the answer. The point of view of a housewife is of no interest whatsoever for the male producers she had contacted. With Miguel Gasòliba, she has the suspicion that had the monologue been a play between the two women, especially with a sexy love scene in it — visually powerful of course — Miguel Gasòliba would have liked it. She was almost sure of it. She rushed out of the office, otherwise she would have killed him.

"I feel like going home and doing some Tai-Chi..." she thinks as she is coming down the Montjuich staircase of the National Palace. Montserrat arrives and runs toward her.

Anna is really upset. As the sun sets, both women stay for a while in the dramatically beautiful Montjuich between sculptures and water fountains. All of Barcelona is at their feet. Montserrat listens to Anna's furious comments about Miguel Gasòliba. Finally Anna throws the copies of her monologue at a garbage can.

"Good-bye to my opening in Barcelona. Now my only chance is San Francisco."

They both were unaware of what was happening at the same time at their apartment. A fax was coming from San Francisco, California. One of the companies was offering Montserrat a position in their research department. Reyna Sion, the Human Resources V.P., signed the letter and it was clear not only that they were impressed with her presentation but also that they were familiar with Montserrat's published articles.

Once they enter the living room, Montserrat realizes that there is a fax. "Come here!"

"What!"

"Look! Look. Look."

Actually, the fax machine is not located in the most convenient position. In order to pick up a fax one had to adopt the strangest positions over the sofa, tear off the fax, stand up again and sit down on the sofa to read its content. Instead of that, when in a hurry, they would kneel directly over the arms of the sofa and from that position read the fax. That is exactly what they do at the present time with the fax addressed to Montserrat.

"San Francisco! It's for you! You got a job! That's wonderful. You got a job!"

"Yeah . . ."

The San Francisco area has several companies with seismic analysis research. It seems obvious now to Anna, but she never linked that the headquarters of Another Stage are in a city also known for its seismic activity.

Anna becomes paranoid. She is not surprised at all by Montserrat's success but the people at Another Stage were not getting back to her. Would they pick up her monologue or not? She decides to give them a call even though calling from Spain overseas is excruciatingly expensive. "I sent the videotape to you people and I need to know when you are going to answer. *Love Thy Neighbor* is the title of the play — the monologue."

Both women try to hide their anxiety about a more than probable separation. Montserrat got what she was longing for for such a long time — a job in research. Only a year ago, the news would have been simply terrific. Today, though, the fact that accepting the job means parting ways with Anna makes her receive the news with reservation. Anna has helped her so much in so many ways that she values their relationship above anything else.

Anna, by all means, tries to be strong. They are

on the bed, their favorite place to hold important conferences. Anna plays with the fax that Montserrat received. The tour-guide-turned-graphologist has already studied Reyna Sion's personality through her signature. She makes the wildest comments about it, but this is not what Montserrat wants to hear.

"Stop it!" replies Montserrat. "OK, now, when are you going to hear from San Francisco?"

"They're going to fax me in a week."

"So what do we do in the meantime? Take a vacation and say a prayer . . . no, say a prayer and take a vacation."

"Where shall we go? Bahamas? Hoboken?"

"No, one more."

"Hoboken is fine."

"Costa Brava."

"Costa Brava?"

"Costa Brava," replies Montserrat leaning over Anna.

Chapter 17

They stroll by Cala S'Alguer where they get excellent views of Platja Castell and the always remarkable Iberic ruins. They had a very good trip and now the key factor is to know how to enjoy themselves while trying to think the minimum. They like the small fishermen's houses. One day, Montserrat wants to have one. They are really small, just one room and the ceiling is curved.

Montserrat has problems with one of her shoes and she sits down and takes the sand out of it. Soon after, Anna appears. Anna has taken an interest in photography. Using Montserrat's camera, she photographs anything from baby waves against the rocks at the floor level, to the rich texture of the rocky walls. These activities bore her in the end.

She looks at the sea and then she turns around to find Montserrat. Montserrat sits on top of a rock. Anna must climb to where she is. Anna is not an archetype of elegance and grace but she does what she can climbing her way up to where Montserrat is.

What is impossible for Anna is to stop thinking. "When we get back to Barcelona, I'd better have a fax from Another Stage in San Francisco waiting for me, a fax saying, 'Yes darling we want you on the Tour.' That way we could stay together. I can hardly imagine my life without Montserrat."

They have gotten used to each other. Their life in common is not the extent of their problems but they both have a lot to lose if a separation takes place. For Anna, Montserrat is by no means a "distraction" but a very positive force that brings out the best in her.

Once Anna arrives to where Montserrat sits, Montserrat caresses her. That is Montserrat's way to gratify Anna for the Herculean effort she made to climb up to where Montserrat sits.

They walk toward the pine trees. There are some sailboats far away and the area seems deserted. The Tramuntana wind does not blow and the day is bright and sunny. Anna carries a blanket. Montserrat tries to get the blanket from Anna, and they both finish in circles with Montserrat holding Anna in her arms. Anna does not like this attention in a public space. Anna protests; she knows what is going on inside Montserrat.

"Now she wants to make love in the middle of nowhere. That's her pattern, whenever she's upset, she wants to make love; whenever I'm upset, I wanna have a pizza," Anna reasons.

As the day passes by, though, Anna cares less and less about being seen. When they finally arrive at the fishermen's houses, they sit together with some equilibrium on their part on top of a rock in front of the tiny houses. At this time of the year, broom and poppies grow all over. The blue of the sea and the green of the pines get complimented now with the yellow tones of the broom and the vivacious red of the poppies.

Anna suddenly realizes Montserrat has a very small insect in her blouse. The sudden movement of Montserrat alerted by the existence of the insect makes them lose the equilibrium. It is time to move on.

Montserrat is really in a romantic mood and she makes Anna feel the same way. They contemplate the immense Platja Castell at their feet while lying on the ground by a small tree. Anna explains everything she knows about the immensity they have in front of them. "That would make a terrific meditation spot," Anna thinks.

Later in the afternoon they embrace by some enormous rocks at Cala S'Alguer. Anna holds Montserrat by the waist while Montserrat has her arm around Anna's neck. Anna starts clowning around. Montserrat holds Anna's head with her arms as Anna holds Montserrat tighter.

It is particularly sad to pass by the same places where they met for the first time. Anna sees the tree where she asked Montserrat if she could give her a

116

kiss. At this precise spot, Montserrat now poses a delicate question. She verbalizes what they both think but only she gathers the courage to speak.

"Anna, do you think we will always be together?"

"I'll think one way or the other we'll always be together."

"I'm praying for that."

They have found a terrific rocky area practically in the middle of the sea. Anna sits and Montserrat has her head on Anna's lap. Anna caresses Montserrat's dark hair as she remembers the long way they have both come. Anna thinks about the day when Montserrat called her up to break up and ended up moving in with her. She remembers: her problems with the red panties; her "cleaning sessions" when she would throw all the dust over Montserrat (who did not notice it); the celebration of the third month anniversary with the dramatic opening of the Champagne; and when Montserrat found the photos of Marta L. Puig. All these images pass through Anna's mind as she fears that Montserrat is on a very similar wavelength.

The Costa Brava will always be a very intimate part of their lives. Anna recalls the passionate first encounter they had right after that first kiss. Then she wanted to die because she felt she would never feel as happy again in her life. She has had quite a number of passionate moments in her relationship with Montserrat since then. More importantly, a true friendship built up. They are lovers and yet terrific friends and companions.

All these memories get suddenly interrupted by Montserrat's velvet voice, "I think I'm getting used to the Tramuntana wind."

They move toward the pine trees. Surrounded by pine needles, Montserrat is about to get what she has been looking for. Anna sleeps. Montserrat picks up her exclusive car key holder and starts passing it over Anna's forehead. Anna awakens. Montserrat keeps passing the car key holder over Anna's face and lips. Finally Montserrat brings it toward her own lips. The expression on her face leaves no doubts as to where she would like to go next.

They enter their car parked at Cala S'Alguer, their usual place. The wild waves crashing against the rocks are the only romantic soundtrack they have. They spend the next hour inside the car. Anna agrees with Montserrat that making love is a terrific way to stop thinking.

The following days are slight variations on the same kind of activities of their first day, plus they take automatic black and white photographs of the two of them. In a particular picture Montserrat looks like she is in a romantic mood whereas Anna looks "cold like a fish." It could not be any other way.

Back in Barcelona, as soon as they enter the apartment, the telephone rings. Anna could not care less. Montserrat rushes toward the telephone, and she picks it up. "Hello? Oh. Hi Jordi." She does not seem very excited to hear him.

"Yes I'm going to San Francisco. Well it's not for a while. Yeah, can we make it lunch instead?"

Another Stage should have answered by now.

There is no fax for Anna from Another Stage. During the next few hours, Anna looks at the fax machine more often than she should. Her anxiety increases by the second. She needs the fax, and she needs to be accepted in the tour. It is not so much the need of performing her monologue, but her desire to be with Montserrat.

Montserrat collects her dry clothes that hang on the terrace, and she notices that Anna sits at the windowsill. Anna has an envelope in her hands.

"Hi," says Montserrat.

"Hi."

"What's the matter?"

"What you mean?" Anna tries not to cry.

"Is there something wrong?"

"No."

"What's that?"

"Oh, that's for you."

"For me? Well give it to me." Montserrat takes it and looks at its contents. "Oh, no. No. I don't want your money."

"It's not my money. It's just money."

"Whose money is it then?"

"Who cares? Take it. I'd like you to take it."

"No, you said we would always be together. You take it."

"No. Montserrat, there's many ways to be together, OK, please take it." Anna, with a broken voice, goes back inside. The fax machine has received no fax from San Francisco.

Anna and Montserrat are at Saint Paul Hospital, for Anna shows it to the tourists. Anna looks pale and so does Montserrat. While the group takes pictures, both women sit on a bench. At their feet, they have pine needles like at the Costa Brava.

"Please pack and go to San Francisco, you'll lose your job," says Anna.

Montserrat does not even want to hear about packing. Anna leaves the bench to take the tourists to the next stop. Montserrat is now always with Anna. She also gets on the bus. Anna addresses herself to the tourists beneath the Columbus statue by the Ramblas. Her voice is sad, all her push and energy long gone.

"Well ladies and gentlemen, we're about to start the tour. Welcome to Costa Brava Tours."

The preoccupation and fear they both feel makes them get very close to losing their tempers. Once they get to Gaudí's Casa Batlló, Montserrat and Anna start arguing.

"Go home and pack."

"Anna, I got enough..."

"You've always got enough when you don't wanna hear what you have to hear. Go home, and pack."

"Anna I'm not going alone, you said we would always be together."

"Let me wait for the fax. You'll lose your job."

"Anna, I don't like this..."

They ignore the fact that all her comments are taped by the tourists' video cameras. As they get to Casa Milà in Passeig de Gracia, Anna has an idea. She will make an effort to share the idea with Montserrat in the most convincing way. She will try anything to get Montserrat to pack and not to lose her job.

"I'll tell you what. I'll join you in San Francisco,

in a couple of weeks. If I don't get the fax, I'll come anyway. I'll go back to Hispanic advertising in the U.S., OK? It's perfect, so please, pack and go, please." Anna does not really know what else to say to Montserrat. Montserrat is stubborn and will not pack. Anna knows that she must go to San Francisco or else they will both regret it for the rest of their lives. Anna tries to push it harder.

"I'll come in two weeks. Would I lie to you? I love you. Please go pack."

Montserrat does not trust Anna's words. By now Montserrat knows her like nobody else has ever known her, not even Marta. What if Anna does not come? What if it is one of Anna's lies?

Anna looks at her audience. She makes some painful considerations. What if she has to accept that she will never have any audience other than the tourists? That could be a possibility, but she knows that when somebody has to let go of something it is just a little bit painful at the beginning and then it turns to relief. Whereas for her to give up acting would be almost like killing her. What if she already had played the role that she had to play in Montserrat's life? They had both grown. They had fun and that is it, *finito*. Maybe that is life; that is why they say that life is a bitch after all.

Anna addresses herself to the tourists at Gaudí Avenue. "Now before we go back to the hotel I would like to make just a couple of comments. First is the way you pronounce 'Barcelona.' "

Montserrat does not want to leave Anna. She has made up her mind. The months they have spent together have been by far the best of her life. She knows that Anna often says the same thing.

"Go pack. I'll come in two weeks. Please."

Convinced that Anna will do as she says, Montserrat sells the car and packs. The money, the plane ticket... she hopes that something will go wrong and she will have to postpone the trip. She gets a terrific plane ticket at once, though, and finds herself a very convenient place to stay in San Francisco.

The telephone rings. It is not a fax. It is a long distance call from San Francisco. It is for Montserrat. Reyna Sion, from her new job, is calling. Far from being excited, Montserrat is about to cry. "Yes, yes I'll be there Thursday at five. Yeah, it's nice of you to say that. Yes, very happy. OK. OK... Thanks Mrs. Sion. OK. Bye." She hangs up and goes for a walk.

Anna finally breaks down. Sitting at the dining room sofa by the fax and playing nervously with a small ball, Anna cries. She knows they will part ways. Anna goes to church.

She notices at first a stunning stained glass window showing Moses pointing toward the promised land. Her crying disturbs two women in front of her who pray the rosary. "No way will I go back to advertising. I've lost her. Please God help me. I love her, please." She looks at the Moses stained glass window.

At the same time, at home, a fax comes through her fax machine. It is from Another Stage. They finally communicate to Anna their decision about *Love Thy Neighbor*. The monologue has been accepted to participate in the U.S. tour. Anna has to be in San Francisco soon. She will go to the U.S. with Montserrat.

When Anna gets back to the apartment,

Montserrat has not come back yet. She cries in the dining room. She closes the window. After a while, she sits down on the sofa and she decides to look at the fax machine.

A loud scream is heard around the whole neighborhood. She has seen the fax from Another Stage. One thousand images appear in her mind. The first one is her adored housewife. It comes to her mind the particular exit that her character makes in a certain part of the monologue. The housewife is sitting in her chair when she thinks she has heard a fax coming through her neighbor's fax machine. She says,

"That's the fax! Sorry, that's the chicken, that is my chicken!"

There are so many things to do and so little time! Anna picks up her blue umbrella and leaves the apartment. She knows where to find Montserrat, but first she has something else to do.

She runs, she cries, and she ruminates on her way to Saint Paul Hospital, "What a miracle. We'll make it together to the U.S. and we'll start a new life, together." Anna is going to find Anna Jr. at the hospital. It could not be a more spectacular sight. From Saint Paul Hospital, the Temple of the Sagrada Familia can be seen. Anna finds her assistant at the entrance of the hospital. Anna gives her a blue umbrella. Anna Jr. will take over. They embrace and Anna Jr. says her goodbyes.

Anna runs toward Gaudí Avenue. One thing she does not want to leave in Barcelona is all of the automatic camera black and white photographs of

Montserrat and Anna, their very own family album. Coincidentally, in the pictures, both women are always by the car having one crisis or another. They will miss that red car. Now new horizons open up in front of them in San Francisco. "I've always suspected there was a God, now I know there's one. And it's a Goddess, fifty percent Catholic and fifty percent Jewish. And she understands Catalan people."

At Gaudí Avenue, she finds Montserrat. "Guess what?" says Anna. Montserrat cannot tell. "Guess what?" asks Anna again.

"What happened?" Montserrat says, concerned.

"I'm . . . coming . . . I'm coming with you to San Francisco," says Anna.

They embrace right in the middle of Gaudí Avenue. Anna for once, could not care less about the bystanders. They kiss. Both are sure now that they will not part ways, that they will see quite a lot of each other for a while. Montserrat feels happy and equally relieved.

It is not over then, their particular love story. She knows that it all started at the wild Costa Brava, several months ago. Anna did not know how to address Montserrat and Montserrat did not know how to address Anna. Anna was the tour guide and Montserrat was a client.

The second time they went to the Costa Brava, they both desired to know more of each other. Montserrat remembers that casual embrace to protect her from the Tramuntana wind. Anna had to take the first step — which she hates — and asked Montserrat's permission to kiss her. Montserrat knows how much she wanted her to do it. Anna wanted to see the effect of such a silly request. The effect was terrific. The kiss led to an hour-and-a-half intimate encounter inside the red car parked under the pine trees of Cala S'Alguer while the Tramuntana blew. This is the memory Montserrat wants to keep of Costa Brava. The third time they went up there, the idea of a more than probable parting of the ways shadowed the vacation.

Montserrat takes Anna by the hand, and realizing that they do not have a second to lose, they run toward the Sagrada Familia on their way to the apartment.

Anna is again the all-energetic, hopeful person she used to be. In the U.S. she will make her dreams come true and so will Montserrat. They both are exultant.

Anna already has plans. "As soon as we get to San Francisco, I'll start getting information about engineers without frontiers, just in case Corporate America disappoints sensitive Montserrat. And as soon as I get to New York City with my monologue, I'm gonna buy myself a sesame bagel with cream cheese at the bagel store on 110th and Broadway."

As they pass by the Temple of the Sagrada Familia, Anna realizes, "One thing I'm sure of, is that we're both gonna miss Barcelona, and Girona . . . and the Costa Brava."

COSTA BRAVA by Marta Balletbo Coll. 144 pp. Read the book,
see the movie!   ISBN 1-56280-153-8 $11.95

MEETING MAGDALENE & OTHER STORIES by
Marilyn Freeman. 144 pp. Read the book, see the movie!
                                                  ISBN 1-56280-170-8   11.95

SECOND FIDDLE by Kate Calloway. 208 pp. P.I. Cassidy James'
second case.   ISBN 1-56280-169-6   11.95

LAUREL by Isabel Miller. 128 pp. By the author of the beloved
Patience and Sarah.   ISBN 1-56280-146-5   10.95

LOVE OR MONEY by Jackie Calhoun. 240 pp. The romance of
real life.   ISBN 1-56280-147-3   10.95

SMOKE AND MIRRORS by Pat Welch. 224 pp. 5th Helen Black
Mystery.   ISBN 1-56280-143-0   10.95

DANCING IN THE DARK edited by Barbara Grier & Christine
Cassidy. 272 pp. Erotic love stories by Naiad Press authors.
                                                  ISBN 1-56280-144-9   14.95

TIME AND TIME AGAIN by Catherine Ennis. 176 pp. Passionate
love affair.   ISBN 1-56280-145-7   10.95

PAXTON COURT by Diane Salvatore. 256 pp. Erotic and wickedly
funny contemporary tale about the business of learning to live
together.   ISBN 1-56280-114-7   10.95

INNER CIRCLE by Claire McNab. 208 pp. 8th Carol Ashton
Mystery.   ISBN 1-56280-135-X   10.95

LESBIAN SEX: AN ORAL HISTORY by Susan Johnson.
240 pp. Need we say more?   ISBN 1-56280-142-2   14.95

BABY, IT'S COLD by Jaye Maiman. 256 pp. 5th Robin Miller
Mystery.   ISBN 1-56280-141-4   19.95

WILD THINGS by Karin Kallmaker. 240 pp. By the undisputed
mistress of lesbian romance.   ISBN 1-56280-139-2   10.95

THE GIRL NEXT DOOR by Mindy Kaplan. 208 pp. Just what
you'd expect.   ISBN 1-56280-140-6   10.95

NOW AND THEN by Penny Hayes. 240 pp. Romance on the
westward journey.   ISBN 1-56280-121-X   10.95

HEART ON FIRE by Diana Simmonds. 176 pp. The romantic and
erotic rival of *Curious Wine*.   ISBN 1-56280-152-X   10.95

DEATH AT LAVENDER BAY by Lauren Wright Douglas. 208 pp.
1st Allison O'Neil Mystery.   ISBN 1-56280-085-X   10.95

YES I SAID YES I WILL by Judith McDaniel. 272 pp. Hot
romance by famous author.   ISBN 1-56280-138-4   10.95

FORBIDDEN FIRES by Margaret C. Anderson. Edited by Mathilda
Hills. 176 pp. Famous author's "unpublished" Lesbian romance.
                                       ISBN 1-56280-123-6   21.95

SIDE TRACKS by Teresa Stores. 160 pp. Gender-bending
Lesbians on the road.   ISBN 1-56280-122-8   10.95

HOODED MURDER by Annette Van Dyke. 176 pp. 1st Jessie
Batelle Mystery.   ISBN 1-56280-134-1   10.95

WILDWOOD FLOWERS by Julia Watts. 208 pp. Hilarious and
heart-warming tale of true love.   ISBN 1-56280-127-9   10.95

NEVER SAY NEVER by Linda Hill. 224 pp. Rule #1: Never get involved
with . . .   ISBN 1-56280-126-0   10.95

THE SEARCH by Melanie McAllester. 240 pp. Exciting top cop
Tenny Mendoza case.   ISBN 1-56280-150-3   10.95

THE WISH LIST by Saxon Bennett. 192 pp. Romance through
the years.   ISBN 1-56280-125-2   10.95

FIRST IMPRESSIONS by Kate Calloway. 208 pp. P.I. Cassidy
James' first case.   ISBN 1-56280-133-3   10.95

OUT OF THE NIGHT by Kris Bruyer. 192 pp. Spine-tingling
thriller.   ISBN 1-56280-120-1   10.95

NORTHERN BLUE by Tracey Richardson. 224 pp. Police recruits
Miki & Miranda — passion in the line of fire. ISBN 1-56280-118-X   10.95

LOVE'S HARVEST by Peggy J. Herring. 176 pp. by the author of
Once More With Feeling.   ISBN 1-56280-117-1   10.95

THE COLOR OF WINTER by Lisa Shapiro. 208 pp. Romantic
love beyond your wildest dreams.   ISBN 1-56280-116-3   10.95

FAMILY SECRETS by Laura DeHart Young. 208 pp. Enthralling
romance and suspense.   ISBN 1-56280-119-8   10.95

INLAND PASSAGE by Jane Rule. 288 pp. Tales exploring conven-
tional & unconventional relationships. ISBN 0-930044-56-8   10.95

DOUBLE BLUFF by Claire McNab. 208 pp. 7th Carol Ashton
Mystery.   ISBN 1-56280-096-5   10.95

BAR GIRLS by Lauran Hoffman. 176 pp. See the movie, read the book! ISBN 1-56280-115-5 10.95

THE FIRST TIME EVER edited by Barbara Grier & Christine Cassidy. 272 pp. Love stories by Naiad Press authors. ISBN 1-56280-086-8 14.95

MISS PETTIBONE AND MISS McGRAW by Brenda Weathers. 208 pp. A charming ghostly love story. ISBN 1-56280-151-1 10.95

CHANGES by Jackie Calhoun. 208 pp. Involved romance and relationships. ISBN 1-56280-083-3 10.95

FAIR PLAY by Rose Beecham. 256 pp. 3rd Amanda Valentine Mystery. ISBN 1-56280-081-7 10.95

PAYBACK by Celia Cohen. 176 pp. A gripping thriller of romance, revenge and betrayal. ISBN 1-56280-084-1 10.95

THE BEACH AFFAIR by Barbara Johnson. 224 pp. Sizzling summer romance/mystery/intrigue. ISBN 1-56280-090-6 10.95

GETTING THERE by Robbi Sommers. 192 pp. Nobody does it like Robbi! ISBN 1-56280-099-X 10.95

FINAL CUT by Lisa Haddock. 208 pp. 2nd Carmen Ramirez Mystery. ISBN 1-56280-088-4 10.95

FLASHPOINT by Katherine V. Forrest. 256 pp. A Lesbian blockbuster! ISBN 1-56280-079-5 10.95

CLAIRE OF THE MOON by Nicole Conn. Audio Book —Read by Marianne Hyatt. ISBN 1-56280-113-9 16.95

FOR LOVE AND FOR LIFE: INTIMATE PORTRAITS OF LESBIAN COUPLES by Susan Johnson. 224 pp. ISBN 1-56280-091-4 14.95

DEVOTION by Mindy Kaplan. 192 pp. See the movie — read the book! ISBN 1-56280-093-0 10.95

SOMEONE TO WATCH by Jaye Maiman. 272 pp. 4th Robin Miller Mystery. ISBN 1-56280-095-7 10.95

GREENER THAN GRASS by Jennifer Fulton. 208 pp. A young woman — a stranger in her bed. ISBN 1-56280-092-2 10.95

TRAVELS WITH DIANA HUNTER by Regine Sands. Erotic lesbian romp. Audio Book (2 cassettes) ISBN 1-56280-107-4 16.95

CABIN FEVER by Carol Schmidt. 256 pp. Sizzling suspense and passion. ISBN 1-56280-089-1 10.95

THERE WILL BE NO GOODBYES by Laura DeHart Young. 192 pp. Romantic love, strength, and friendship. ISBN 1-56280-103-1 10.95

FAULTLINE by Sheila Ortiz Taylor. 144 pp. Joyous comic lesbian novel. ISBN 1-56280-108-2 9.95

OPEN HOUSE by Pat Welch. 176 pp. 4th Helen Black Mystery. ISBN 1-56280-102-3 10.95

ONCE MORE WITH FEELING by Peggy J. Herring. 240 pp.
Lighthearted, loving romantic adventure.   ISBN 1-56280-089-2   10.95

FOREVER by Evelyn Kennedy. 224 pp. Passionate romance — love
overcoming all obstacles.   ISBN 1-56280-094-9   10.95

WHISPERS by Kris Bruyer. 176 pp. Romantic ghost story
                                ISBN 1-56280-082-5   10.95

NIGHT SONGS by Penny Mickelbury. 224 pp. 2nd Gianna Maglione
Mystery.   ISBN 1-56280-097-3   10.95

GETTING TO THE POINT by Teresa Stores. 256 pp. Classic
southern Lesbian novel.   ISBN 1-56280-100-7   10.95

PAINTED MOON by Karin Kallmaker. 224 pp. Delicious
Kallmaker romance.   ISBN 1-56280-075-2   10.95

THE MYSTERIOUS NAIAD edited by Katherine V. Forrest &
Barbara Grier. 320 pp. Love stories by Naiad Press authors.
                                ISBN 1-56280-074-4   14.95

DAUGHTERS OF A CORAL DAWN by Katherine V. Forrest.
240 pp. Tenth Anniversay Edition.   ISBN 1-56280-104-X   10.95

BODY GUARD by Claire McNab. 208 pp. 6th Carol Ashton
Mystery.   ISBN 1-56280-073-6   10.95

CACTUS LOVE by Lee Lynch. 192 pp. Stories by the beloved
storyteller.   ISBN 1-56280-071-X   9.95

SECOND GUESS by Rose Beecham. 216 pp. 2nd Amanda Valentine
Mystery.   ISBN 1-56280-069-8   9.95

A RAGE OF MAIDENS by Lauren Wright Douglas. 240 pp. 6th Caitlin
Reece Mystery.   ISBN 1-56280-068-X   10.95

TRIPLE EXPOSURE by Jackie Calhoun. 224 pp. Romantic drama
involving many characters.   ISBN 1-56280-067-1   10.95

UP, UP AND AWAY by Catherine Ennis. 192 pp. Delightful
romance.   ISBN 1-56280-065-5   9.95

PERSONAL ADS by Robbi Sommers. 176 pp. Sizzling short
stories.   ISBN 1-56280-059-0   10.95

CROSSWORDS by Penny Sumner. 256 pp. 2nd Victoria Cross
Mystery.   ISBN 1-56280-064-7   9.95

SWEET CHERRY WINE by Carol Schmidt. 224 pp. A novel of
suspense.   ISBN 1-56280-063-9   9.95

CERTAIN SMILES by Dorothy Tell. 160 pp. Erotic short stories.
                                ISBN 1-56280-066-3   9.95

EDITED OUT by Lisa Haddock. 224 pp. 1st Carmen Ramirez
Mystery.   ISBN 1-56280-077-9   9.95

WEDNESDAY NIGHTS by Camarin Grae. 288 pp. Sexy
adventure.   ISBN 1-56280-060-4   10.95

SMOKEY O by Celia Cohen. 176 pp. Relationships on the
playing field.   ISBN 1-56280-057-4   9.95

KATHLEEN O'DONALD by Penny Hayes. 256 pp. Rose and
Kathleen find each other and employment in 1909 NYC.
                                        ISBN 1-56280-070-1   9.95

STAYING HOME by Elisabeth Nonas. 256 pp. Molly and Alix
want a baby . . . or do they?   ISBN 1-56280-076-0   10.95

TRUE LOVE by Jennifer Fulton. 240 pp. Six lesbians searching
for love in all the "right" places.   ISBN 1-56280-035-3   10.95

KEEPING SECRETS by Penny Mickelbury. 208 pp. 1st Gianna
Maglione Mystery.   ISBN 1-56280-052-3   9.95

THE ROMANTIC NAIAD edited by Katherine V. Forrest &
Barbara Grier. 336 pp. Love stories by Naiad Press authors.
                                        ISBN 1-56280-054-X   14.95

UNDER MY SKIN by Jaye Maiman. 336 pp. 3rd Robin Miller
Mystery.   ISBN 1-56280-049-3.   10.95

CAR POOL by Karin Kallmaker. 272pp. Lesbians on wheels
and then some!   ISBN 1-56280-048-5   10.95

NOT TELLING MOTHER: STORIES FROM A LIFE by Diane
Salvatore. 176 pp. Her 3rd novel.   ISBN 1-56280-044-2   9.95

GOBLIN MARKET by Lauren Wright Douglas. 240pp. 5th Caitlin
Reece Mystery.   ISBN 1-56280-047-7   10.95

LONG GOODBYES by Nikki Baker. 256 pp. 3rd Virginia Kelly
Mystery.   ISBN 1-56280-042-6   9.95

FRIENDS AND LOVERS by Jackie Calhoun. 224 pp. Mid-
western Lesbian lives and loves.   ISBN 1-56280-041-8   10.95

THE CAT CAME BACK by Hilary Mullins. 208 pp. Highly
praised Lesbian novel.   ISBN 1-56280-040-X   9.95

BEHIND CLOSED DOORS by Robbi Sommers. 192 pp. Hot,
erotic short stories.   ISBN 1-56280-039-6   9.95

CLAIRE OF THE MOON by Nicole Conn. 192 pp. See the
movie — read the book!   ISBN 1-56280-038-8   10.95

SILENT HEART by Claire McNab. 192 pp. Exotic Lesbian
romance.   ISBN 1-56280-036-1   10.95

THE SPY IN QUESTION by Amanda Kyle Williams. 256 pp.
4th Madison McGuire Mystery.   ISBN 1-56280-037-X   9.95

SAVING GRACE by Jennifer Fulton. 240 pp. Adventure and
romantic entanglement.   ISBN 1-56280-051-5   10.95

CURIOUS WINE by Katherine V. Forrest. 176 pp. Tenth Anniversary Edition. The most popular contemporary Lesbian love story.
                                        ISBN 1-56280-053-1   10.95
        Audio Book (2 cassettes)   ISBN 1-56280-105-8   16.95

CHAUTAUQUA by Catherine Ennis. 192 pp. Exciting, romantic
adventure.   ISBN 1-56280-032-9   9.95

A PROPER BURIAL by Pat Welch. 192 pp. 3rd Helen Black
Mystery.   ISBN 1-56280-033-7   9.95

SILVERLAKE HEAT: A Novel of Suspense by Carol Schmidt.
240 pp. Rhonda is as hot as Laney's dreams.   ISBN 1-56280-031-0   9.95

LOVE, ZENA BETH by Diane Salvatore. 224 pp. The most talked
about lesbian novel of the nineties!   ISBN 1-56280-030-2   10.95

A DOORYARD FULL OF FLOWERS by Isabel Miller. 160 pp.
Stories incl. 2 sequels to *Patience and Sarah.*   ISBN 1-56280-029-9   9.95

MURDER BY TRADITION by Katherine V. Forrest. 288 pp. 4th
Kate Delafield Mystery.   ISBN 1-56280-002-7   11.95

THE EROTIC NAIAD edited by Katherine V. Forrest & Barbara
Grier. 224 pp. Love stories by Naiad Press authors.
                                                ISBN 1-56280-026-4   14.95

DEAD CERTAIN by Claire McNab. 224 pp. 5th Carol Ashton
Mystery.   ISBN 1-56280-027-2   10.95

CRAZY FOR LOVING by Jaye Maiman. 320 pp. 2nd Robin Miller
Mystery.   ISBN 1-56280-025-6   10.95

STONEHURST by Barbara Johnson. 176 pp. Passionate regency
romance.   ISBN 1-56280-024-8   9.95

INTRODUCING AMANDA VALENTINE by Rose Beecham.
256 pp. 1st Amanda Valentine Mystery.   ISBN 1-56280-021-3   10.95

UNCERTAIN COMPANIONS by Robbi Sommers. 204 pp.
Steamy, erotic novel.   ISBN 1-56280-017-5   9.95

A TIGER'S HEART by Lauren W. Douglas. 240 pp. 4th Caitlin
Reece Mystery.   ISBN 1-56280-018-3   9.95

PAPERBACK ROMANCE by Karin Kallmaker. 256 pp. A
delicious romance.   ISBN 1-56280-019-1   10.95

THE LAVENDER HOUSE MURDER by Nikki Baker. 224 pp.
2nd Virginia Kelly Mystery.   ISBN 1-56280-012-4   9.95

PASSION BAY by Jennifer Fulton. 224 pp. Passionate romance,
virgin beaches, tropical skies.   ISBN 1-56280-028-0   10.95

STICKS AND STONES by Jackie Calhoun. 208 pp. Contemporary
lesbian lives and loves.   ISBN 1-56280-020-5   9.95
Audio Book (2 cassettes)   ISBN 1-56280-106-6   16.95

UNDER THE SOUTHERN CROSS by Claire McNab. 192 pp.
Romantic nights Down Under.   ISBN 1-56280-011-6   9.95

GRASSY FLATS by Penny Hayes. 256 pp. Lesbian romance in
the '30s.   ISBN 1-56280-010-8   9.95

A SINGULAR SPY by Amanda K. Williams. 192 pp. 3rd
Madison McGuire Mystery.   ISBN 1-56280-008-6   8.95

THE END OF APRIL by Penny Sumner. 240 pp. 1st Victoria
Cross Mystery. ISBN 1-56280-007-8   8.95

KISS AND TELL by Robbi Sommers. 192 pp. Scorching stories
by the author of *Pleasures*. ISBN 1-56280-005-1   10.95

STILL WATERS by Pat Welch. 208 pp. 2nd Helen Black Mystery.
ISBN 0-941483-97-5   9.95

TO LOVE AGAIN by Evelyn Kennedy. 208 pp. Wildly romantic
love story. ISBN 0-941483-85-1   9.95

IN THE GAME by Nikki Baker. 192 pp. 1st Virginia Kelly
Mystery. ISBN 1-56280-004-3   9.95

STRANDED by Camarin Grae. 320 pp. Entertaining, riveting
adventure. ISBN 0-941483-99-1   9.95

THE DAUGHTERS OF ARTEMIS by Lauren Wright Douglas.
240 pp. 3rd Caitlin Reece Mystery. ISBN 0-941483-95-9   9.95

CLEARWATER by Catherine Ennis. 176 pp. Romantic secrets
of a small Louisiana town. ISBN 0-941483-65-7   8.95

THE HALLELUJAH MURDERS by Dorothy Tell. 176 pp. 2nd
Poppy Dillworth Mystery. ISBN 0-941483-88-6   8.95

SECOND CHANCE by Jackie Calhoun. 256 pp. Contemporary
Lesbian lives and loves. ISBN 0-941483-93-2   9.95

BENEDICTION by Diane Salvatore. 272 pp. Striking, contemporary romantic novel. ISBN 0-941483-90-8   10.95

TOUCHWOOD by Karin Kallmaker. 240 pp. Loving, May/
December romance. ISBN 0-941483-76-2   9.95

COP OUT by Claire McNab. 208 pp. 4th Carol Ashton Mystery.
ISBN 0-941483-84-3   10.95

THE BEVERLY MALIBU by Katherine V. Forrest. 288 pp. 3rd
Kate Delafield Mystery. ISBN 0-941483-48-7   11.95

THE PROVIDENCE FILE by Amanda Kyle Williams. 256 pp.
2nd Madison McGuire Mystery. ISBN 0-941483-92-4   8.95

I LEFT MY HEART by Jaye Maiman. 320 pp. 1st Robin Miller
Mystery. ISBN 0-941483-72-X   10.95

THE PRICE OF SALT by Patricia Highsmith (writing as Claire
Morgan). 288 pp. Classic lesbian novel, first issued in 1952 . . .
acknowledged by its author under her own, very famous, name.
ISBN 1-56280-003-5   10.95

SIDE BY SIDE by Isabel Miller. 256 pp. From beloved author of
Patience and Sarah. ISBN 0-941483-77-0   10.95

STAYING POWER: LONG TERM LESBIAN COUPLES by
Susan E. Johnson. 352 pp. Joys of coupledom. ISBN 0-941-483-75-4   14.95

SLICK by Camarin Grae. 304 pp. Exotic, erotic adventure.
ISBN 0-941483-74-6   9.95

NINTH LIFE by Lauren Wright Douglas. 256 pp. 2nd Caitlin
Reece Mystery.   ISBN 0-941483-50-9   9.95

PLAYERS by Robbi Sommers. 192 pp. Sizzling, erotic novel.
                                            ISBN 0-941483-73-8   9.95

MURDER AT RED ROOK RANCH by Dorothy Tell. 224 pp.
1st Poppy Dillworth Mystery.   ISBN 0-941483-80-0   8.95

A ROOM FULL OF WOMEN by Elisabeth Nonas. 256 pp.
Contemporary Lesbian lives.   ISBN 0-941483-69-X   9.95

THEME FOR DIVERSE INSTRUMENTS by Jane Rule. 208 pp.
Powerful romantic lesbian stories.   ISBN 0-941483-63-0   8.95

CLUB 12 by Amanda Kyle Williams. 288 pp. Espionage thriller
featuring a lesbian agent!   ISBN 0-941483-64-9   9.95

DEATH DOWN UNDER by Claire McNab. 240 pp. 3rd Carol
Ashton Mystery.   ISBN 0-941483-39-8   10.95

MONTANA FEATHERS by Penny Hayes. 256 pp. Vivian and
Elizabeth find love in frontier Montana.   ISBN 0-941483-61-4   9.95

LIFESTYLES by Jackie Calhoun. 224 pp. Contemporary Lesbian
lives and loves.   ISBN 0-941483-57-6   10.95

WILDERNESS TREK by Dorothy Tell. 192 pp. Six women on
vacation learning ''new'' skills.   ISBN 0-941483-60-6   8.95

MURDER BY THE BOOK by Pat Welch. 256 pp. 1st Helen
Black Mystery.   ISBN 0-941483-59-2   9.95

THERE'S SOMETHING I'VE BEEN MEANING TO TELL YOU
Ed. by Loralee MacPike. 288 pp. Gay men and lesbians coming out
to their children.   ISBN 0-941483-44-4   9.95

LIFTING BELLY by Gertrude Stein. Ed. by Rebecca Mark. 104 pp.
Erotic poetry.   ISBN 0-941483-51-7   10.95

AFTER THE FIRE by Jane Rule. 256 pp. Warm, human novel by
this incomparable author.   ISBN 0-941483-45-2   8.95

PLEASURES by Robbi Sommers. 204 pp. Unprecedented
eroticism.   ISBN 0-941483-49-5   9.95

EDGEWISE by Camarin Grae. 372 pp. Spellbinding
adventure.   ISBN 0-941483-19-3   9.95

FATAL REUNION by Claire McNab. 224 pp. 2nd Carol Ashton
Mystery.   ISBN 0-941483-40-1   10.95

IN EVERY PORT by Karin Kallmaker. 228 pp. Jessica's sexy,
adventuresome travels.   ISBN 0-941483-37-7   10.95

OF LOVE AND GLORY by Evelyn Kennedy. 192 pp. Exciting
WWII romance.   ISBN 0-941483-32-0   10.95

CLICKING STONES by Nancy Tyler Glenn. 288 pp. Love
transcending time.   ISBN 0-941483-31-2   9.95

SOUTH OF THE LINE by Catherine Ennis. 216 pp. Civil War
adventure.   ISBN 0-941483-29-0   8.95

WOMAN PLUS WOMAN by Dolores Klaich. 300 pp. Supurb
Lesbian overview.   ISBN 0-941483-28-2   9.95

THE FINER GRAIN by Denise Ohio. 216 pp. Brilliant young
college lesbian novel.   ISBN 0-941483-11-8   8.95

BEFORE STONEWALL: THE MAKING OF A GAY AND
LESBIAN COMMUNITY by Andrea Weiss & Greta Schiller.
96 pp., 25 illus.   ISBN 0-941483-20-7   7.95

OSTEN'S BAY by Zenobia N. Vole. 204 pp. Sizzling adventure
romance set on Bonaire.   ISBN 0-941483-15-0   8.95

LESSONS IN MURDER by Claire McNab. 216 pp. 1st Carol Ashton
Mystery.   ISBN 0-941483-14-2   10.95

YELLOWTHROAT by Penny Hayes. 240 pp. Margarita, bandit,
kidnaps Julia.   ISBN 0-941483-10-X   8.95

SAPPHISTRY: THE BOOK OF LESBIAN SEXUALITY by
Pat Califia. 3d edition, revised. 208 pp.   ISBN 0-941483-24-X   10.95

CHERISHED LOVE by Evelyn Kennedy. 192 pp. Erotic Lesbian
love story.   ISBN 0-941483-08-8   10.95

THE SECRET IN THE BIRD by Camarin Grae. 312 pp. Striking,
psychological suspense novel.   ISBN 0-941483-05-3   8.95

TO THE LIGHTNING by Catherine Ennis. 208 pp. Romantic
Lesbian 'Robinson Crusoe' adventure.   ISBN 0-941483-06-1   8.95

DREAMS AND SWORDS by Katherine V. Forrest. 192 pp.
Romantic, erotic, imaginative stories. ISBN 0-941483-03-7   10.95

MEMORY BOARD by Jane Rule. 336 pp. Memorable novel
about an aging Lesbian couple.   ISBN 0-941483-02-9   12.95

THE ALWAYS ANONYMOUS BEAST by Lauren Wright Douglas.
224 pp. 1st Caitlin Reece Mystery.
                                        ISBN 0-941483-04-5   8.95

MURDER AT THE NIGHTWOOD BAR by Katherine V. Forrest.
240 pp. 2nd Kate Delafield Mystery.   ISBN 0-930044-92-4   11.95

WINGED DANCER by Camarin Grae. 228 pp. Erotic Lesbian
adventure story.   ISBN 0-930044-88-6   8.95

PAZ by Camarin Grae. 336 pp. Romantic Lesbian adventurer
with the power to change the world.   ISBN 0-930044-89-4   8.95

These are just a few of the many Naiad Press titles — we are the oldest and
largest lesbian/feminist publishing company in the world. We also offer an
enormous selection of lesbian video products. Please request a complete
catalog. We offer personal service; we encourage and welcome direct mail
orders from individuals who have limited access to bookstores carrying our
publications.